LOST IN THE STORM

A WAR WITHIN A WAR

Kevin Willis

KEVIN WILLIS

LOST IN THE STORM

A WAR WITHIN A WAR

By: Kevin D. Willis

email: bluehd1200@live.com

phone: (334)-414-3958

address: 150 Knight Drive

Wetumpka, AL 36092

BOULEVARD BOOKS
The New Face of Publishing
www.BoulevardBooks.org

ISBN 13 978-1-942500-54-4

INTRODUCTION

It was almost midnight and an exceptionally dark night with no moon out. The car pulled up the driveway of the small farmhouse in the rural outskirts of Ilam.

Alammahad Shannabidad, an Iraqi terrorist group leader in the north region of Iraq stepped out of his car. Alammahad was to be meeting with an Iranian General, General Aveev. After the appropriate greetings were made, they entered the small farmhouse that was to be used for their secret meeting.

General Aveev was the biggest illegal arms dealer to the terrorists in Afghanistan and had recently become an unknown supplier to the Iraqi terrorists as well.

Aveev was meeting with Shannabidad to strike a deal on the sale of some much needed weapons and munitions for the Iraqis ongoing conflict with the Americans.

After they came to an agreement on price and form of payment General Aveev told his new partner that his first delivery would arrive in five days.

Shannabidad said that he was looking forward to a long and fruitful future with the General and showed him to the door. Aveev returned to his hotel room in Ilam where he made a phone call. He organized the shipment of the requested items, then had his men readied for what was usually, a routine job.

2

CHAPTER 1

"THE CRASH"

I t was March 12, 2008. US forces had been in Iraq since the beginning of time, or so it seemed.   In all actuality it'd been seven, long, and painfully unproductive years.   Sergeant Keith A. Williams was part of the 275th Engineering Battalion.

The 275th Engineering Battalion was responsible for route clearance in central Iraq.   The US military had all but taken over the country completely.

Osama Bin Laden was an anti-American terrorist in Afghanistan and leader of the Taliban, a largely detested terrorist group in Afghanistan.   He had orchestrated a high scale attack on the United States with the aid of Sadam Hussein who was, at the time of the attacks the Dictator / President of Iraq.

Following the attack of the United States, and the World Trade Center on September 11, 2001, US forces invaded Iraq and Afghanistan. It was rumored that U.S. forces had found and assassinated Bin Laden. They soon captured Sadam Hussein.   Hussein was tried and convicted on multiple counts of murder and a plethora of other charges.   He was found guilty on all counts, sentenced, and hanged to death in his own country.

The plan was to assist in the reconstruction of the Iraqi government but the country was still full of religious radicals and terrorist followers still loyal to their past leaders.

This posed a big problem for the American Military because they had to put up with attacks from these separatist groups while trying to rebuild this disestablished country that a greedy, arrogant, dictator had run into the ground. In order to reestablish order in Iraq these insurgents were going to have to be weeded out and disposed of.

Sergeant Williams was part of, one of many Units deployed to Iraq to assist in these efforts. He had been in Iraq for eight long months and was finally going to get a break. He was scheduled to go on his two week leave and could hardly wait. He was so excited. He had been away for so long he was starting to wonder if his two little girls would even remember who he was.

He was a young man at only thirty-two years old and had been in the Army National Guard for nine years. He was about 5'11", brown hair, blue eyes, medium build, not a bad looking guy. He had a six year old and a two year old daughter.

His wife had left him as soon as she found out about his deployment. It had been pretty tough on him at first but after a while he sort of just accepted the fact that it was over and decided it was best to just focus on the future and his two girls and move on. Those girls were all he had now and they meant the world to him.

The war on terrorism had been an ongoing ordeal for so long that the American people were really just tired of it to say the least. Trying to rebuild a government in a country that never really had much of one to start with was proving to be a more difficult task than they had expected it to be. The Americans didn't want to be there and the locals weren't thrilled with us living in their back yards either.

The US didn't seem to be making a great deal of progress there and to make matters worse Iran was beginning to make some bold moves themselves. It had been rumored that Iraq's neighbors were being friendly neighbors but it became much clearer how friendly when they got caught red handed selling bombs to the bad guys. The Iranian Government had denied all accusations of their involvement in the exchanges.

The Iranian President, Mahmoud Ahmadinejad had openly blamed the U.S. and/or the U.K. governments for several bombings that had killed Iranian military forces in Zahedan and Ahvaz in the southern regions of Iran. Although the war was between the U.S. and Iraq, tensions had still grown between Iran and the west over the last few years.

On top of all of that the Presidential Elections were coming up and no-one could decide who to vote for. Did you vote for the guy that wanted to take all the troops out of Iraq, because clearly everyone was tired of being there?   Did you vote for the one that wanted to stay, because it was smart to keep our forces close to Iran, or what?

At the time, all Sergeant Williams knew, was he couldn't wait to get home for a little R&R.   He was so close he could taste mama's cookin' and smell the scent of the pine trees that grew all around where he lived in the little town of Waterville, AL.   All he had to do was not miss his flight and he was home free for 14 days.

It was three A.M. Thursday morning, *or was it Friday.   The days all seem to run together here,* thought Sergeant Williams as he stepped out of the Humvee into the loosely packed gravel at the PAX terminal. That's where the GI's and civilian contractors fly in and out from at the Airbase there in Balad, Iraq.   *"Thursday, Friday, I really don't care as long as I get on that plane and get out of this place,"* he thought to himself as he grabbed for his gear In the back seat.

"Have fun, but don't get into any trouble while your home.   I'll see you back here in a couple of weeks all right sarge!" yelled Specialist Massey over the roar of the diesel engine.

"Ahh, you know me I don't get in trouble Mass, but ok I'll see ya in couple weeks!" he shouted back.   He slammed the door and turned to face the building.   His thoughts were interrupted by the thundering blast of an F-18 fighter jet rocketing into the night sky as they so often did at the busy Airbase.   There were always at least two fighters in the air at all times.   This was so that if there was ever a need they could be easily dispatched to the target location.   Williams had spent countless, restless nights listening to the jets as they made their regular, mundane, take-offs at all hours of the night.

The PAX terminal was a long metal building with tall concrete barriers all the way around it with a narrow gap between two of the towering pillars right in the center of the building.

"C'mon man!   All flights are leavin early cause a sand storm's comin'!" yelled a soldier who nearly ran over Sergeant Williams as he rushed inside.

Williams looked down at his watch.3:07....."Oh shit!" he said out loud.   "My flight's at 3:20."

The last few soldiers walked out the opposite side of the building onto the tarmac as he was walking in.   He broke and ran but halfway across the room he heard, "Whoa there hotshot.   Tarmac's off-limits right now.   When's your flight?"

Fighting to catch his breath Williams barked out,"03:20, flight C-20973PYO!"

"Easy now buddy that flight left outta here a half hour ago, but not to worry there are about twelve more guys down at the end there that missed the same one."   He pointed to the far wall where a dozen frustrated individuals were huddled grumbling and cursing aloud.

"Just go down there and wait.   I'll be there in a few minutes to let you know what's up, ok?" the man said still pointing.

"Thank you sir," he muttered as he turned and headed toward the other end of the terminal.   "Could things get any worse?" he thought.

"I hate this stupid desert," someone bellowed.

"Yeah, me and you both," he returned.

"Now what?" asked another Soldier.

"Just be patient," said a young Lieutenant by the name of David Gadsby.

"Hey," came a deep, but friendly voice behind Sergeant Williams. He turned to find himself face to face with about a two hundred and seventy pound black man with a slightly receding hairline.   "I'm Buford but everybody just calls me BB."

Buford Boatwright was originally from Chicago but had been living in Texas for the last six years where he had been laid off from his job with a local trucking company.   He had answered an ad in his local paper for a company called KBR (Kellog, Brown, & Root).   The ad had promised good benefits and excellent pay only he'd have to go to Iraq to get it. He was single, jobless, and he really didn't have any close related family so he applied and was quickly hired due to the scarcity of volunteers.

"I'm Keith but everybody calls me Sergeant" Williams said with a grin. "Are you excited about going home?"

8

The big guy chuckled "I sho am! I'm so tired of this place. Man you just don't know."

Williams laughed," Are going home to stay or just a visit?"

He wrinkled his brow," You kiddin? I'd be out of my mind not to come back for this easy money."

"I wish I could say the same," Williams said with a smile. "Not only do we not get the choice whether to come or not, the pay is shitty too."

They waited for what seemed like forever and the civilian guy that had stopped him earlier finally came down and informed them that they were still able to arrange a flight for them.

It was a smaller plane but it would actually save them some time because it would fly straight to Germany instead of going south to Kuwait first.   In fact, he told them that it would really be better because they would not have to lay over in Kuwait like everyone else and they should be flying home the next day if not that same night.

After about another half hour or so they were escorted out to the plane they would be hitching a ride with.

The C-130 cargo plane was sitting on the tarmac and was lit up like a Christmas tree.   The lights would be turned off as soon as they lifted off and turned back on after they reached normal flying altitude. The planes were instructed to do so in order to decrease visibility for anyone who may attempt to shoot an anti-aircraft rocket at a plane leaving the Base.

The plane had dual engines on each wing and the large cargo doors were opened all the way up like a giant garage door. The young Lieutenant mumbled to himself as they walked to the plane, "I hate flying." Williams, who was walking in front of the Lieutenant smiled at his nervousness and without responding turned to see who had made the statement. He had ridden on plenty of C-130's in his career so he wasn't the least bit concerned about getting on this one.

After they were all loaded up and were being taxied out to the runway he began to take mental inventory.

There were three civilian contractors, two female Army soldiers, eight male Army soldiers, and, he had only seen two Air Force guys.

"Surely it takes more than two people to fly a C-130." he asked the crew guy, who answered,

"Oh don't worry. We do this all the time. Besides we will be getting two additional guys in Germany." He gave a nod of understanding and sat back in his seat to buckle in.

The C-130 was lined on both sides with net seats and the cargo hold was empty because this was actually the return trip for the Air Force guys.

Once on the runway the pilot raced the engines. One of the

engines on the right side choked out and he had to restart it twice. The Lieutenant looked at Sergeant Williams and said with great sarcasm, "Well, doesn't that make you feel confident?" Williams had been on C-130's so many times that he knew that was perfectly normal and there was nothing to worry about. Or was there?

Williams noticed that as usual everyone had voted to sit in the rear of the plane with hopes that once they were clear of the storm the pilot would open the cargo doors which they will sometimes do when they aren't carrying any cargo. He thought of how disappointed they were going to be because he knew that there were strict restrictions on the opening of the cargo doors over combat areas.

The only people that sat in the front were the civilians except one he was more interested in flirting with the females. Williams and the Lieutenant also sat in the front section of the plane.

Williams had never met the Lieutenant. He didn't recognize him at least. The Lieutenant was dark headed, real tall and thin. He worked as a logistics officer in a Finance Company. Lieutenant Gadsby was from Virginia and was engaged to be married when his deployment was over. He was a full time National Guardsman and was a finance officer back in the states also.

BB was sitting next to the Lieutenant. The other guy's name was Mike Kelly who was an electronics engineer and he probably weighed 130 pounds soaking wet with rocks in his pockets, and was almost bald.

Mike had taken an early retirement and had worked as an independent contractor for several big companies but was really just bored.   A friend had told him about the job in Iraq as a civilian contractor and persuaded him to go with him.   They'd only been in country for three weeks when his friend's mother became ill and Mike was left there by himself.

The pilot came over the mic and told them the trip would take about two and a half hours after wheels up.   *"Just a few more hours,"* he thought, *"A few more hours and I'll be on a commercial flight out of Germany, headed for the continental US and in less than 24 hours I'll be sitting at home with my family."*

Williams looked across the aisle at Lieutenant Gadsby.   He had beads of sweat forming on his brow and he had his elbows propped on his knees, hands together as if in prayer.

"Nervous?" Williams asked.

"I get that way when I fly," Gadsby answered.

"Don't worry I've been on plenty of these birds and I've never had any real problems."

"Thanks," he said, still not sure.

He and the Lieutenant talked for what seemed like hours and occasionally Mike would add a word or two to the conversation. Suddenly, it felt as if the plane just fell straight out of the sky.   The Lieutenant's face was struck with terror.   Williams assured him it was only a pocket of much denser air and that it was perfectly normal.

The single crewman came back from the cockpit to tell them that they would be experiencing some brief turbulence not to worry. The Airman nearly fell as he turned to go back to the cockpit and the plane lurched a second time this time more to the side and not as short lived.

BB, who was very much awake all of a sudden grumbled, "Yeah, we noticed."

Williams had a bad feeling.   Something wasn't right. Something didn't sound right.   The sound of the engines had changed but not like they do when they land, no, this sound was new.   After he could no longer stand it, curiosity got the best of him and he got up.   He worked his way toward the middle of the plane where he knew a small window was located.

What he saw when he looked out he was all but prepared for. Thick, black smoke was billowing from the outside engine and he was almost certain he could see flames within the thick streaks of black and grey.   It seemed as though every time the beacon light on the wingtip would flash the plume of smoke was larger and thicker than the time before.   His stomach sank and a chill ran down his spine.   Suddenly he found himself fighting back panic.

He turned and purposefully made his way toward the front but not so fast as to draw a lot of attention.   The last thing they needed was a full scale panic at 20,000 ft.   He went into the cockpit area and immediately asked the pilot, "Do you realize that we have a fire on the right wing?"

The pilot looked at Williams and said, "Soldier, a blown engine is the least of our worries at the moment."

"What do you mean?" he asked.

The pilot turned to face Williams and said, "We don't know where we are."

"What do you mean?" "You don't know where we are!" Williams almost shouted too loudly.

"We're dead in the air." the pilot said.

"Dead in the air?" he asked.
"We have lost all navigational capabilities, all SATCOM, and all radio communication, and we've been flying blind for about an hour."

"Why do I have a feeling that's not even the worst news?"

"Well, Sergeant we're scheduled to run out of fuel.....as he checked his wrist.....ten minutes ago."

"Can you emergency land this bird?" Williams asked, fearing the worst in his answer.

"For all I know we could be less than 1000ft off the ground already.   If I can't see through the dark the best I can do is take her down slow and hope we're somewhere over open desert or water."

Williams swallowed the lump in his throat and said, "Then I suggest you start hoping now," and pointed to a light on the panel board that was flashing (LOW OIL PRESSURE).

Williams and the lone Airman returned to the cargo bay. Williams took his seat and started to buckle up his hands were shaking and the Lieutenant asked, "Is everything ok?"

Williams didn't want to start a panic but felt an obligation to give them fair warning so he said, "Just do your seat belt and hang on.   It's about to get rough."   The crewman called for everyone's attention.

"Attention! Attention, everyone.   We are going to be making an emergency landing.   Please secure all loose objects and ensure that your lap belts are tight and secure.   Please remain seated until the aircraft has come to a complete stop."   BB, Mike and the Lieutenant all looked at Williams wide-eyed and pulled their belts tight.   Williams leaned his head back and held on to the rail that the net seats were attached to. BB was trying to quote the Lord's Prayer and Mike and the Lieutenant were both looking around with fear of what was about to happen.

Lieutenant Gadsby looked at a picture of Jessica his fiancé and gave it a quick kiss.   He looked at BB who was still praying aloud and Mike was already panicking and saying, "Oh God, oh God, oh God. The crewman, after checking everyone's belt, disappeared back into the cockpit and just seconds later it happened.

The plane hit with a force like he'd never felt before.   The right wing hit first plowing through the sand like a giant knife and slammed the nose violently into the ground.   The plane plowed forward until apparently finding something solid where it then toppled end over end.

After the first flip the fuselage was torn into as if it were made of tin foil.   The rear section of the plane turned sideways and went into a roll dissevering the wings and scattering their remains in a trail of debris. The rear section now wingless and rolling came to rest on the remaining front section of the plane.

It had finally come to a halt and was half buried, nose first in sand and gravel at the base of what looked like a small mountain.   The opening where the body of the plane had been snapped into was pinched back together as if to reseal itself from the outside air.

The rear half of the fuselage was on fire but not yet engulfed in flames.   It was teetering back and forth as though it would continue rolling if it wasn't blocked by the first section of the tattered aircraft.

The stabilizers and tailfin were left back where the wings had been ripped away and was still intact but laying over sideways with one stabilizer and the tailfin on the ground and the other stabilizer at about 45 degrees skyward.

Somehow Sergeant Williams found himself a good 20 or 30 meters from the wreckage and sore but as far as he could tell unscathed. He scrambled to his feet and gathered himself.   He then worked his way slowly back toward the aircraft, careful to search the rubble as he went.

The first body he came to was lifeless and still under what looked to be a part of one of the engines.   He tried to remove the debris but it was too heavy for him alone.

He knelt beside the soldier and felt for a pulse.   There was nothing.   He fought back tears and pressed onward toward the wreckage.

The nose of the plane looked like a coke can that someone had emptied and stepped on to crush it like an accordion.   As he climbed into the fuselage he saw several mangled and disfigured bodies lying within the wreckage.   He thought for a moment he was going to be sick but was interrupted by cries for help from somewhere close by.

He noticed a foot moving from the other side of a row of seats still attached to each other but seemingly ripped from the center of the plane.   He remembered that just moments ago he'd been strapped securely to one of those seats.   Would he have survived if his seatbelt had held?   Who knew?   He shook his head to regain his train of thought.

When he got to the person crying for help he found that it was Mike Kelly, the contractor that had been sitting right next to him.   His left arm was tangled in the net seating and was most definitely broken, probably in several places.

"Hold on Mike. I'm gonna get you out ok."

"My arm!" he cried out in agony. "It's broken."

"I'm going to cut you free." Williams assured him.

He remembered a knife that he had put in a hidden pocket of his bag that always made it past customs.   He finally found his bag and retrieved the knife.

The net was tightly wound around Mikes arm and Williams thought for a moment how was it even possible for this to have happened, but once again snapped out of it and began to cut Mikes arm free from the nylon netting.

After several minutes of cutting and Mike howling he was free. Williams took a piece of stiff plastic out of his backpack that had been used to support the bag and made a perfect splint.   He secured the splint on Mikes arm and asked him if he could help him.

"I need you to see if you can find a medic bag or just any kind of medical supplies.   Look for anything with the medical cross insignia on it."

"Where are you going?" Mike asked like a child afraid his mother was going to leave him standing alone in the middle of a busy supermarket.

"I'm going to see if I can find anyone else and I'll also be looking for supplies myself."

"Ok," Mike said, reluctantly.

After sending Mike to search for supplies Williams continued his search for survivors.   He called out, "Can anyone hear me!" as he crawled deeper into the belly of the plane.

It was still dark and it was very difficult to see.   He remembered the flashlight that he kept on his belt and he recalled looking at it that very morning and considering leaving it there to lighten his load. He thought to himself, *"I sure am glad I kept it."*

As he dug through the debris he thought he heard something. "Hello!" he cried. "Can you hear me?" He heard a faint cry for help from somewhere deep beneath the tangled web of twisted metal, electrical wiring, and conduit. "Hello! Keep talking so I can follow your voice," he said while throwing a piece of wrinkled sheet metal out of his way.

"I'm here, please, my leg......it's.......stuck, please, hurry."

"I'm gonna get you out," Williams said. "Don't you worry." He scraped and dug until finally he found the trapped victim.

It was Lieutenant Gadsby. "Hey sir, it's me, Sergeant Williams. Are you hurt?"

"I'm not sure," he grunted. "I can't feel my leg. I think the circulation is cut off."

Williams climbed over him to get a better look. A full section of one of the cargo doors had somehow ended up on top of the Lieutenants right leg. There was a lot of blood but he couldn't really tell what kind of damage was done until he could get the door of his leg and pull him out of there. "I'll be right back I promise. I am going to need a hand to get you out of here."

As Sergeant Williams made his way back out of the tunnel he'd made through the debris he was cutting and pulling electrical wires as he went. He would use these wires to make a rope of sorts to use and pull the injured Lieutenant out of the wreckage where he was trapped.

"Mike!" he yelled as he emerged from the wreckage.

"I'm here!" answered Mike as he carefully worked his way through the mayhem to Williams' location.

"I'm gonna need a hand.   Follow me."

Back at the entrance to where the Lieutenant was he said, "Ok Mike, tie this around your waist and when I say pull, you pull with all you got, Understand?"

"Got it" Mike said as he inspected the multi-colored, multi-strand bundle of wires he'd been handed.

Sergeant Williams wormed his way back to Lieutenant dragging the improvised rope he'd gathered on his way out just minutes before.

Once he got to the Lieutenant he said, "I'm going to loop this around you and when I lift up on the door you try and help drag yourself out, roger?"

"Roger," groaned the Lieutenant.

"Ok, on three. One.....two........three!   Ok Mike, pull!"   The wires pulled tight. After several grunts and groans he was free, but he wasn't happy.   The feeling came back like a tidal wave.

Lieutenant Gadsby was moaning in pain and Williams felt as if there was nothing he could do.   His leg had been severely crushed and Williams wondered if he may even end up losing it by the looks of it.

He was bleeding profusely but it didn't look like arterial bleeding so Williams applied pressure and wrapped it up tight with bandages from a medical bag that Mike had found in what used to be the cockpit. Remembering his first aid training, he started an IV from the medical kit to replace some of the blood that the Lieutenant had lost.   Then he said, "We need something to make a crutch or something with."

"Why would he need a crutch?" asked Mike.

"Well, unless you would rather carry him?"

"Why don't we just wait here for someone to find us?" suggested Mike.

"Well," continued Williams, "First of all we don't even know where we are. We don't know if anyone else knows where we are or who might find us first. Judging by the direction...." Suddenly they were interrupted.

"Hello!" was heard from somewhere close to the cockpit.

As they worriedly approached the mangled cockpit, much to their surprise and amazement, it was BB and he was without even a scratch.

"You lucky son-of-a-bitch," raved the Lieutenant.   "Not one scratch.   Mike breaks his arm, I get my leg crushed and you don't get a damn scratch."

BB chuckled a little. "Guess I'm just lucky like that.   Know what I mean?   What about you Sarge?   You get hurt?" asked BB with squinted eyes.

Williams realized he'd not even thought to check and see if he was injured. He noticed a sharp pain in his back and it felt as though there was something sticky running down his back. As he inspected himself, he noticed that he had a pretty significant cut on his lower back but he shrugged it off and played it off as nothing more than a scratch.

"Oh that's nothing, just a scratch, I'm fine." Something caught his eye toward the barely recognizable cockpit. It was the pilot's M9mm pistol and belt.

"Sir," he said as he headed toward the cockpit. "It may be in our best interests to be prepared for the worst."

"What do you mean?" asked Gadsby.

"Well......."

As he started to speak he noticed something unusual. It was a tire. Not a tire from the plane. No, this tire came off a truck, but where was the rest of the truck? He had a terrible feeling that the ground was not the only thing that they had hit when they fell from the sky that morning.

"See if you can find anything that looks like it didn't come from the plane." he shouted.

"What exactly do you expect to find?" asked the Lieutenant.

"I'm not sure. I just know that tire didn't come off a C-130." He pointed at the tire, flat, but still mounted on a once black rim, now rusted and considerably weathered. The tire itself although it was flat, looked

22

fairly new with little wear. Something wasn't adding up here.

Lieutenant Gadsby looked around as best he could with his leg bound up in the makeshift splint Williams had put on it.   BB sat down and wished he'd listened to Nana Truman, the woman who he thought of as the closest person to being his mother, when she had told him not to take the job with KBR.   He also wished he'd packed more to snack on as his stomach grumbled and growled in agreement.

Mike was griping and complaining about the heat and saying aloud, "Why in the world did I let Jim talk me in to coming to this Godforsaken Country."

He was about to start on a new grievance when he froze stiff.

"Hey Sarge, Are you looking for something like that perhaps?" he shouted back over his shoulder, not taking his eyes of his target.

The group gathered behind Mike to visually investigate his discovery. Under the rear section of the plane which had smoldered out was a large truck that was undoubtedly used for transporting supplies and such.

The front grill was protruding ever so slightly out from under the burning pile of rubble that was once the tailfin and upper section of the plane's cargo hold.

As they made their way through the wreckage to where the truck was buried and on its right side, they noticed that it was Iranian military. There were still two Iranian soldiers inside the box cab of the truck.

Williams approached cautiously to inspect and evaluate the situation.   He checked the passenger for a pulse.   There was none.

The driver was pinned between the seat and the steering wheel. He reached to see if he could free the lifeless body and when he moved the body his head moved revealing the shards of glass protruding from his neck.   His lips were dark blue and his arm which Williams quickly let go of was ice cold already.

"They're definitely dead," he said as he backed out of the mangled vehicle.   He thought aloud, "They couldn't have been out here all by themselves." as he walked around to the underside of the truck.

"Maybe they were lost or something." suggested BB as he stumbled and tried to keep up with Williams.

"No, these were two uniformed, Iranian, soldiers.   They wouldn't have been out here driving through the desert without at least one escort truck for security."

"Yeah," agreed the Lieutenant.   "There has to be another truck around here somewhere."

They began to search for any clues or evidence that there had been another truck accompanying the unfortunate travelers.

"If they were looking to start a war, looks like they were on the right track," BB announced as he peered into a box that had apparently come from the back of the truck.

Williams shuffled over to help BB investigate.   There were several boxes scattered in the trucks' vicinity. The first one he looked in was full of RPG's (Rocket Propelled Grenades). RPG's are used abundantly by the Iraqi insurgents against US forces which was Williams first thought when he saw them. "This don't look good." He said worriedly.

As they inspected the rest of the boxes, one contained AK-47 assault rifles and ammunition. Another had plastic explosives and several more had more AK-47 ammo in them. The Lieutenant asked, "I wonder where they were going with all this stuff?"

"And who it was intended to be used on?" Williams added.

"As I was saying before we found BB, judging by the direction of the debris trail, we were coming from that direction." He pointed northwestward with a dirty, bloody finger. "So considering the amount of time we were in the air and direction of travel I'd place us somewhere deep inside the Iranian border."

"Great!" growled Mike, "Out of the pot, and into the frying pan. So, where do we go if we don't stay here?"

Lieutenant Gadsby spoke up, "I'm with him," pointing at Williams. "I say we head west back toward Iraq. At least we know there are American forces there."

Mike fussed, "Do you know how far it must be? It'd be suicide!" BB interrupted and asked, "Shouldn't it be light out by now?" Williams looked at his watch, then at the sky. BB was right. It looked like that sand storm was still going strong and it was headed their way.

"Looks like a sand storm, and a bad one," the Lieutenant noted. "I vote we stay the storm out in the front end of the plane.   It's the sturdiest structure we've got and I don't really see any other options." Everyone agreed and they huddled into the shell of the plane as deep as they could to wait it out.

The storm came like a hurricane without the water.   The sand burned as the wind blasted them with it.   They completely covered themselves to keep the sand from eating through their skin like a sand blaster.

For hours the winds roared around them and they spent the better part of the day in total darkness.   They settled in for a long wait and eventually each of them fell sound asleep, entombed, in a blanket of sand and dust.

CHAPTER 2

"THE AFTERMATH"

"How in the hell, do you lose a C-130 cargo plane and why did I hear that it left this base without refueling?" shouted Major Haffick.

Major Richard Haffick was responsible for overseeing all Air Force air travel over and around Iraq. He was 43 years old and the hair that he had left was still mostly dark with a touch of gray sprinkled throughout.

"We didn't lose it sir, it just......just....it just disappeared." said the Airman First Class nervously. He was one of the air traffic controllers on duty the night that flight C-20973PYO left the Air Base northbound for Germany.

"Cargo planes... last time I checked don't do disappearing acts and what about the fuel?" demanded Major Haffick.

The Airman First Class said, "The pilot convinced the tower that he had enough..."

"Wait just a damn minute!" interrupted Major Haffick. "Do you try to drive twelve hundred miles on half a damn tank of gas?"

"Hell, I think I'll just drive home from work today with my hood up! I might even let the air out of a couple of the tires. Does that sound like a good idea? Does it Airman?" By this point his whole face is red and everyone in the room was trying to avoid eye contact.

Outside the room the post Commander, Two Star General Hubert Omar, and some his staff had arrived for an emergency meeting.

General Omar was with the fifth Infantry Division. He had served in the US Army for thirty-three years. He'd served in every conflict that the United States had been in during his thirty-three years of service. He had done his longest tour in the Gulf War when he was on orders for all but four months of the entire engagement.

General Omar was all of six foot two and weighed just less than two hundred pounds. There wasn't a hint of grey in his dark, almost black hair and for a fifty-two year old man he was in top-notch physical condition.

He had seen war from both sides and he hated it. He was one of the Army's top ten most decorated officers. He had seen his share of combat action and had even spent several months as a prisoner of war during the Croatian War of Independence.

He had been considering retirement when the terrorist attacks on the United States in 2001 occurred and TRADOC requested him specifically for the job. He reluctantly took the job and he thought to himself as he waited for the Major that this is the very reason he'd been reluctant in his decision to accept the position.

"One moment sir," said a soldier who was standing outside the door of the control room afraid to enter with the Major shouting like he was.

She stuck her head in and nervously interrupted," Major Haffick.......Sir."   He turned to look.   "The General Sir, is here to see you."

"Thank you," he snapped his head back to the Airman First Class. "I'll deal with this matter later, "he promised, and left the room to meet with the General.

In the hallway Major Haffick said, "I wish I could say it's good to see you General, but considering the circumstances....."

"I'm good thank you.   And you?" the General replied.

Major Haffick rolling his eyes and sighing said," I think I'm going to have a nervous breakdown."   As he opened the door to the conference room he said, "After you Sir."

In the conference room the General asked as he took his seat at the end of the long mahogany table," What do we have Major?" "Well," started the Major as he leaned forward, propping both palms on the edge of the table," We know that they had enough fuel for about 2,200 miles. That's barely enough to have gotten them to their destination in Germany."

"Why would they not fuel up before leaving here?" asked the

General already having a pretty good idea what the answer was.

The Major answered, "Well sir, that's an issue that I am going to address and a problem that *will* be eradicated.   Apparently sir, the pilot convinced my ground people and my control tower that they had enough fuel to make their trip."

"Why take the risk?" asked General Omar.   The Major answered, "There was a really bad sand storm on the way sir, and they didn't want to get caught in it.   That's not all though.   They also only had one pilot and one crewman.   The mandatory crew for a C-130 is four."

"There should be a pilot, co-pilot, a navigator, a materials handler, and a spare navigator."

"Well," said the General, "We can't change that at this point so, continue."

"They left here at 04:40 on Thursday, March the 12th." said the Major.   They immediately headed off course and not just a little.   They were nearly 40 degrees off.   Radio contact was lost just as they cleared the runway so if they didn't realize there was a problem they would have had no reason to call the tower."

"They were headed north northeast when we lost them on radar. If they continued on the course that they were on they could be anywhere between here and Turkmenistan."   He walked across the room and pointed to a map on the wall as he spoke.

"Or if they had realized their mistake and attempted to adjust

30

their bearings to get back on course they could be within a two to three thousand square mile area."   He moved his hand east on the map and drew an imaginary circle around the area he was indicating.

As he walked back to his original place at the table the General asked, "What efforts are being made to try and locate the aircraft?"

As he sat the Major replied, "So far satellite imagery has turned up nothing and our people in Turkey are monitoring the waters over the Black Sea for signs of debris but they've also found nothing thus far."

"We can't violate airspace restrictions in certain areas so our hands are tied in some places as far as aerial surveillance but we're doing what we can with those assets as well."

"Are there any suspicions being raised in.... say for instance, Iran, Russia, maybe even Afghanistan?"

"We've got a plate full as it is sir but as far as we can tell, according to our Intel there has been no adverse activity in Iran's military forces and there have been no reports from Afghanistan.

As far as Russia, well, that's a can of worms we'd rather not shake too hard unless we just have no other options."

General Omar leaned back in his chair and sighed as he crossed his legs, rotating his right foot and cracking his ankle.   "I hate to break it to you Major, but if satellite imagery is getting us nowhere and restrictions on airspace are obstructing your efforts, then you just might not have any other options."

One of the general's staff members cleared his throat as if to remind them that he was there and asked. "Do the C-130's not have some sort of tracking devise on them; i.e. a little black box?"

Thinking to himself, *does this idiot really think we would be having this meeting if we could find a tracking beacon*, he answered, "They do but unfortunately and possibly their greatest flaw, the C-130's beacon operates in conjunction with the navigational system of the aircraft.   In light of the fact that we are getting no signal we are assuming that they didn't have any idea where they were and probably did not adjust their course."

The General asked, "Is that all Major?"

"At this time Sir we are exhausting all efforts and as soon as we have more info, Sir, I assure you, you'll be the first man notified."

General Omar stood and said," I'll see what I can do with Russia. You continue to keep a close eye on Iran and keep me posted on any changes in the situation."

"I will sir and thank you for your time." said the Major as he scurried around the table to open the door for the General.

"There are American people missing somewhere out there and for any possible survivors, time is of an essence.   I suggest, Major, you use yours wisely."   As he squatted slightly to grasp the handle of his briefcase, the General used his other hand to push his glasses back onto the bridge of his nose and turned toward the door.

Major Haffick softly speaking as he pushed open the door answered "Yes Sir."

The beam of his flashlight blasted through the darkness like a spotlight as Sergeant Williams looked around.   The sand storm had finally subsided.   He checked his watch, 1:47p.m.

He realized that it should be light out and they were in complete darkness.   His stomach sank. "We're buried," he said aloud.

"Wha...wha...what," mumbled BB.   "What's goin on?   Where we at?" he asked, as he became startled to consciousness.

"It's ok BB," Williams said quietly.   "The storm must have buried us in the sand, but I'm pretty sure we can dig our way out."

"You want me to wake them two up?" he asked, pointing at the other two men huddled in the front of the partial fuselage.

"No, let 'em sleep they'll need all the rest they can get.   Besides, I need you right now to help me."

"What you want me to do?"

Williams looked around as if to access the situation.   Then he looked back at BB, paused a moment, and said,

"Dig."

General Aveev peered out the window of his study where he spent almost all of his free time enjoying the quiet and putting his self on a pedestal, admiring all his accomplishments, wealth and power.

He was, after all, a very prestigious man being a General in the Iranian Army and he lived just as such a man of his position should, in his mansion in Semnan.

The phone on his desk rang. He walked to his desk where he pushed the speaker button as he sat down in his leather button-back, swivel chair.

"Sir, we have a problem." muttered a voice over the phone's speaker.

It was one of his personal men and it definitely didn't sound like a pleasure call. He picked up the phone and placed it to his ear. "What is it?" he asked.

The reply came back," Sir, there's a problem with the shipment."

He stood back up and sternly asked, "What kind of problem?"

"The shipment never showed up at checkpoint one in Kashan." said the voice on the phone. "We had thought perhaps the sandstorm had delayed them but they have had plenty of time now to get here. What would you have me do sir?"

General Aveev said," Take a patrol and check their route. See if they may have had trouble enroot from the bunker."

"Right away sir." replied the voice.

The General kept a stockpile of military weapons cache in a remote, secret storehouse which he referred to as his bunker.   For the last eleven years he'd been stockpiling, skimming off his own government, and dealing with corrupt military officials from all over the world and selling his weapons to terrorist for a hefty profit.

Without putting the receiver down he hung up the phone and checked his recent calls list.   He picked the desired number and released the receiver button.

The phone automatically dialed and was answered after the first ring.   "Sir?" crackled the voice on the phone.

"Prepare another shipment same as yesterdays and take it to the rendezvous point in Ilam."

"Sir, yes sir, right away sir." the voice replied.

Captain Ishbad walked out of the warehouse at the edge of town that they used as a meeting place out of the publics sight to where three of his men were awaiting instructions for their next mission.

He gathered them in a group.   "We are going to the bunker. We will check for signs of the truck along the way.   Move out!"

They loaded into their jeep and sped out of town.

It was approximately three hundred miles from Kashan to the bunker.   It would take them the remainder of the day and on into the night to drive through the vast, uninhabited territory.

The bunker was a fully manned, operational, and fortified compound hidden in the middle of the Dasht-e Kavir (Great Salt Desert). If they didn't find the truck along the way the Captain would gather some extra men while he was at the bunker and form several search parties. He would send the details out to the surrounding villages and towns to search for clues to where the missing truck might be.

He knew he must find the truck quickly because if the wrong people found it the Generals credibility would be greatly at risk and he knew the General would not stand for that.

Captain Ishbad Khorrashmsizar had worked for the General as the ring leader of his illegal supply operation for nine of the eleven years the General had been in business.

Typically, the Captain handled all the Generals dirty work.   He had carried out assassinations of political rivals and executed scores of people throughout the years for the General.

During the conflict between Afghanistan and Iran he'd overseen and at times personally led covert raids on Afghan villages just to keep the conflict alive.   As long as there were ongoing conflicts in and between the surrounding countries business was good for an illegal arms dealer.

The Captain had been discharged from the Iranian Army for a questionable decision made during a bust on a suspected arms dealer years earlier resulting in the arms dealer getting away scot free and was hired by the General fulltime.   His loyalty was unwavering to General Aveev and he had the Generals complete trust.

The General had considered trying to get the charges dropped but rather than bring attention to him-self and risk having more investigations started.   It was easier to just pull some strings and have the Captain discharged honorably.   Then hire him as his personal head of security.

It was a win-win for the both of them.   The Captain proved his loyalty to the General and in turn was given a small army of his own and a position of power which was honorable to those close to him and the General gained a worthy leader to oversee his secret operation for him while he was busy with the actual Iranian Army.   After all in Iran it was a difficult task to find trustworthy followers.   The Captain checked his watch.   It was a quarter past two.   He thought to himself, about five and a half hours from here to the bunker and we need light to look for this truck in the open desert. "   Let's go!" he shouted.   "Keep your eyes open.   It may be hard to see if the sand storm has covered it."

"Yes sir!" they shouted back and leaned from the sides of the jeep

37

as if to get a better look.

The control room was busy as usual with people relaying messages and monitoring screens.   A voice came over the loud speaker, *"Major Haffick please report to the conference room.   Major Haffick please report to the conference room."*

He looked at the clock.   It was already past two.   He suddenly remembered his two 'o clock briefing with the General.   "Oh shit!" he exclaimed.   "Captain, take over for me there's something I have to tend to."

"No problem Sir," the Captain replied.

As he maneuvered his way down the busy hallway through the heavy mid-day traffic of people scurrying to get paperwork done and caffeine cravings tamed he stepped into a side room halfway down the hallway.   "Brown!" he shouted.

"Yeah....s.. Sir," Senior Airman Brown replied noticing who he was talking to.

"Conference room.....now!"

He sprang to his feet, digging through papers and finally finding the folder that he was apparently looking for.   "Yes sir, on my way sir."

As Brown entered the hallway and looked to the right, the Major had already vanished into the conference room. He made his way to the door. He checked his mental note pad to make sure he'd shaved that morning and had a fresh pressed uniform on.

Once he had completed his mental checklist he cautiously entered the conference room. There were five people in the room, all sitting at the table and obviously awaiting his arrival to begin the meeting. "Sorry," he whispered as he sat at the only unoccupied chair left at the table.

His co-worker and coincidentally his roommate also Airman First Class Windom, was sitting directly across from him shook his head slightly and gave a half grin.

"Ok," began Major Haffick. "We believe we know why they lost the Aircraft from radar." He looked at Brown and said, "General, this is Senior Airman Brown. He is our Tracking Systems supervisor and radar systems expert." He looked at brown as if to say, you've got the floor.

Brown started to stand and General Omar motioned with his free hand to sit back down. He held in his other hand an almost empty and probably cold cup of coffee which brown assumed he picked up in their break room on his way there.

"Yes, well," he began, "Normally, radar collected data is in polar coordinates, so conversion from polar coordinates to Cartesian coordinates has to be made first. As we take the position gaps as the input to the neutral network, the value of the input vector has to be a certain range to make sure that the overflow does not happen in the calculation of updating the weights.   Therefore...."

"English... please."   Major Haffick interrupted.   "I don't even understand you, and I have a degree in Aerospace Engineering."

"Yes, uh... sorry.   Uh, w-well, see you uh, the uh...."

Windom leaned forward in his chair from across the table and took over saying, "The AN/SPS-49 radar system operates in the presents of clutter, chaff, and electronic counter-measures."

"We have two of these AN/SPS-49 radar systems.   One of these systems runs in regular operation.   This system tracks mid-range to high flying aircrafts."

"The other AN/SPS-49 runs in what is called 12 RPM mode. This system tracks, or rather detects faster, low flying objects.   Its main purpose is to detect and locate hostile, fast moving targets such as missiles, or enemy fighter jets."

"That'll do," said Major Haffick and promptly took over the conversation.   As the Major began Brown looked across the table at Windom and blew out a breath of relief as a sign of thanks for bailing him out.   Windom gave a quick smile and returned his attention to Major Haffick.

The Major continued, "Just after they went wheels up and lost radio communications, a blip was noted on the radar running in the 12 RPM mode. This was not uncommon and probably ignored as they usually are."

"These blips are usually ignored if they are moving slower than three or four hundred miles per hour and are not moving directly in our direction."

The General gave a look of confusion and asked, "Why are these blips ignored?"

"Well, these blips are usually just predators flying harmlessly around the Airbase and are controlled and monitored by a team of experts elsewhere. You are familiar with the Predator right Sir?"

"Yes of course......"

"No actually," interrupted the suited man sitting next to General Omar.

"Oh! I'm sorry sir, and...." he said turning to look at the rest of the group, "I'm sorry gentlemen. This is Mr. Anthony Patterson. He is the personal advisor to the Secretary of Defense in Washington."

They all nodded hello to each other and Major Haffick stood halfway up so that he could reach to shake his hand. He sat back down and Mr. Patterson reminded Major Haffick, "The Predators?"

Major Haffick continued, "The Predator is an unmanned aerial vehicle (UAV) used mainly for surveillance and reconnaissance. It does however, carry a small arsenal and has what we call Hellfire missiles that have proven themselves to be very useful on several occasions when a firefight has gotten out of hand."

"Anyway back to the radar.   According to the last transmissions that we recovered from that morning, our search area has gotten a little bigger."

"How much bigger?" asked the General.

Major Haffick stood up and started toward the map on the far wall.   On his way by he looked at Brown and said, "That's all we'll be needing from you." then nodded at Windom the same.

Brown and Windom stood to exit the room and Windom shook Mr. Patterson's hand as he walked around the table and made for the door.

The Major pointed at the map as he continued, "We believe there is a possibility that they could have gone as far south as Tehran or anywhere in-between or about 2000 miles past Tehran."

"This complicates things a bit more."   Mr. Patterson said. "If there is the slightest possibility that Iran shot down an American plane, this could very quickly get very ugly."

"Well," said the General, "We really think the plane went down due to mechanical problems, but..."

Mr. Patterson interrupted, "If there is *any* possibility?" He gave the General a look.   The General closed his eyes and nodded a quick nod in silent response.

"I'll brief the Secretary of Defense on my way back to Washington."

"You understand, we must take precaution and prepare for the worst, rather than sitting here, completely unprepared for, whatever."

"I understand," said General Omar.   "Let's just try and avoid jumping to conclusions. The last thing we need is to bring Iran into this war all because of a lack of information."

"Of course," replied Patterson.   "We are only taking precaution as of now. Only precaution."

The General escorted the suits out of the room leaving the Major there alone.   The Major walked back to the map and studied it for a moment.   He let out a sigh and groaned aloud, "Where are you? Where... the hell... are you?"

CHAPTER 3

"THE JOURNEY BEGINS"

They were on the verge of panic at the mere thought of being cooked alive in their nature-made oven.   Then, to their reprise a slither of light cut through the thick darkness of the buried fuselage.

Sergeant Williams' heart nearly jumped from his chest.   He felt as if he could scream with excitement but after hours of labor fully digging and scraping at the sand that had been abundantly heaped atop their hasty-made shelter, he could scarcely even breathe.

As the stale, hot air was replaced with seemingly cool fresh oxygen Mike and the Lieutenant came to life and began shaking and brushing the sand from their clothing.   "At least you guys have boots," whined Mike, as he shook the sand from his tennis shoe.

"Get those," Williams said, pointing to the still half buried body of one of their less fortunate, fellow passengers.   "He doesn't need 'em anymore."

"Your kiddin' right?" replied Mike.

Tired of his complaining as was everyone, Lieutenant Gadsby said, "Just get the damn boots or keep the damn shoes.   Either way, just stop bitching. We're all here, and I'm pretty sure I speak for everyone when I say none of us want to be here."

Mike grimaced and mumbled, "Somebody woke up on the wrong side of the plane."   Williams and BB looked at each other and tried to suppress their laughter.   BB's attempt to hold it back failed slightly and he let slip a bit of a snort.

BB took a moment to regain his composure and said, "What now sarge?"

Williams turned to BB and said, "Give me a hand will ya."
BB locked his fingers together and prepared to give Williams a boost.

The light from the sun was almost unbearable as he climbed from the hole.   He noticed that everything was completely covered or at least from where he stood he could see nothing but an endless sea of sand. He turned his attention back to the hole.

"Ok, send up the supplies and stuff."

After he threw the medical bag aside he turned to find himself staring down the barrel of an AK-47.   "Whoa shit!   Watch where you point that thing." he exclaimed.

"I thought it would be a good idea to get these."   BB said, as he handed up two AK-47's and one RPG tube.

"What kind of ammo did you get?" asked Williams.

45

"I got two boxes of bullets and three of these he said handing up two RPG rounds.

"Careful with those." Williams said as he took one of the rounds. "If we need those we're in trouble, but it's better to be safe than sorry I suppose."   He took the other two rounds and said, "Go ahead and pass me those ammo cans."

After handing up the ammo cans BB reached up as if to shake hands with Williams.   Williams laughed a laugh of disbelief and said, "If you think I am just going to reach in there and pull your big ass out of there, you got another thing comin."

"Mike, you first, then you can help me with those two."   He nodded in gesture to BB and the Lieutenant.

"Careful with my arm," Mike said as he reached up to take Williams' hand.

After pulling Mike up, together, they lifted BB and the Lieutenant out of the buried wreckage.   "Ok," Williams said, "Lieutenant, you carry the pilots 9mm and I'll carry the crewman's.   BB, do you think you could carry the RPG tube and an AK?"

"No problem," BB said as he fought to get the sling of the tube over his head.

The Lieutenant laughed, "You know you can adjust that sling." BB turned to look at the Lieutenant and said,

"I did already."   The Lieutenant raised his eyebrows with a short,

"Oh, my bad."

"That's alright," BB said.   "I might be big but that don't mean I'm slow."   He gave a quick left then a right jab at the air.   Mike rolled his eyes and walked away as if he knew where he was going.

Williams thought to himself, Sure BB, you're a real killer.   Instead he smiled and said, "I know buddy.   That's why I need you to be my biggest helper, ok."

BB smiled and said, "You know I've got your back bro."

The Lieutenant checked the chamber of the 9mm and looking at Williams said, "Ok, so what's the plan."

Williams answered, "I don't know.   You're the Lieutenant."

"Yeah but I don't know anything about the field."

BB broke in and said, "You boys ain't makin' me feel any better 'bout this."   Williams looked at the Lieutenant who looked as if he would break out in tears at any minute.

"All right, where's Mike?" asked Williams.   The Lieutenant turned around to face the same direction as BB and Williams.

BB shouted, "Yo Mike!"

"What?" whimpered Mike.

"You think you would like to join us to see what we're going to do now?" asked the Lieutenant.   Mike trudged through the sand, back to where the other three men stood patiently.

Sergeant Williams knelt down on one knee and repositioned the rifle he'd slung over his shoulder so as to keep the muzzle of the barrel out of the sand that blanketed the ground around them and as far as the eye could see.

"Ok," he began. "Let's start with what we know. We have survived a plane crash and a killer sandstorm and are now lost, somewhere in the middle-east. According to the way the wreckage was strewn we all agree that we came from the west."

"We have minimal supplies as far as food and water is concerned and we have a decent arsenal to protect ourselves from possible hostile threats. Do we agree that hostile forces are a legitimate possibility?" They all three nodded in agreement.

"Do we think we are in Iran or what?" he asked.

The Lieutenant spoke up, "That's a hard one to know, really. All of the countries surrounding Iraq for miles are desert type lands, but according to your prediction before the storm it would be very possible that we're in Iran."

Williams continued, as he shifted to his other knee still ensuring that he didn't stab the muzzle of his weapon into the sand, "We don't have much food at all and we only have enough water for a few days at best."

"Preferably we would want to travel at night because of the lack of heat and simply because if there are hostiles in the area, the dark would provide concealment. There's only one problem with that though."

He didn't wait for a response but continued saying, "If we want to go west-southwest we need to be following the sun.   Trust me I do remember from our land navigation training that a little mistake can turn into miles after you've gone so far."

The Lieutenant facetiously asked, "Did anyone happen to bring a compass?" No one laughed.

"We won't make it a day walking in this heat," lamented Mike. "Besides, how's he going to keep up with that leg?" he asked motioning in the Lieutenant's direction.

Lieutenant Gadsby raised his eyebrows slightly and responded with, "I'd rather die tryin than die lyin."

"What do we have to eat?" asked BB.

Mike stood up astonished that BB could even think of food given their current situation and shouted,

"I don't believe you people!   All he wants' to do is eat.   Mr. Macho here thinks he's going to hop across the desert on a broken leg, and Rambo here just wants to blow something up!"

By now Williams was getting agitated and says, "Whoa, whoa, wait a minute.   What makes you think that I just want to blow something up?"

Lieutenant Gadsby spoke up as Mike was once again walking away to sulk and said, "Sitting here, arguing with one another isn't going to get us out of this mess any faster than we got into it."

BB said, "I didn't mean to piss him off."

Williams looked at BB and said, "It's ok BB.   I know you're hungry.   I am too.   Let's see what we've got."   He walked to where all the supplies are piled in a disheveled stack and pulls a brown box to his feet.

"Have you ever eaten an MRE?"   Williams asked, as if it were a disgrace to have done so himself.

"Yeah," BB replied in the same ignominious tone.   "Meals Ready to Eat." BB chanted sarcastically.   Better than nothin though, right?" he asked.

"Yeah, better than nothing." Williams replied.

"Are you hungry Sir?" Williams asked the Lieutenant.

"Yeah, what do you have?" he asked solemnly.   Williams threw him one of the brown plastic, airtight packages.

"Ooo, beef stew, yum." he said sarcastically.
"I got spaghetti and meat sauce." bragged BB. "Not meatballs, *meat sauce.*   What'd you get Sarge?" he asked curiously looking at Williams' with squinted eyes.

Williams smiled, "I got ravioli."

As the three quietly ate their fine cuisine, Mike came over and grabbed an MRE and walked away to sit alone and eat.

"Wonder why he's so irritable?" asked Lieutenant Gadsby.

"Some people just handle stress differently."   Williams said.

"He'll be all right.   It's not like he has much choice.   Know what I mean?"

"I thought you were going to punch his freakin' lights out for a minute there." said Lieutenant Gadsby.

Williams grinned, "I thought about it."   They all gave a little laugh and finished their meals.

After they'd eaten, Mike came back over and sat down on a case of bottled water and stared into the distance.   His pride prevented him from admitting what they all knew.   That he'd thought it through and he realized that if he didn't cooperate he was just going to make things worse for the whole group.

They loaded all the supplies that they could into the three bags that they had salvaged from the wreckage.   "We'll walk as far as we can before dark and then a few more miles after dark won't hurt too much." Williams said as he heaved the backpack that he had used for his carry-on bag for the flight home.

"Shouldn't we do something about the bodies?" asked Mike.

"What bodies?" asked BB.

"The ones that were on the plane." insisted Mike.

"Like what, bury them?   It looks like Mother Nature saved us the trouble." commented Williams.

"It's already six and it'll be dark by eight so we'd better get a move on." said Lieutenant Gadsby.

"How far you think we'll get before dark?" asked BB.

"I don't know maybe three......four miles. Somethin' like that." answered Williams.

"Everybody keep your eyes peeled.   If you see anything suspicious, inform the rest of us and everyone drop to the ground. Remember, we still don't know how hostile this place is and we should just assume the worst."

"That doesn't mean shoot anything that moves.   That just means everything is a potential threat until we've proven otherwise. Everyone understand?"   Everyone nodded and they began to walk.

They had only walked about 150 meters when Sergeant Williams held up his hand, clinched in a tight fist which everyone recognized as the universal sign for freeze.   He examined the ground in front of him and turned to tell the rest of the group what he'd found.

"Tire tracks," Williams said.   "Two sets.   That definitely tells us that we are not the only people out here."

"Should we follow the tracks?" asked Mike."

"No," said Williams. "We are already assuming that we're in hostile territory.   We need to avoid civilization as best we can."

"He's right." agreed the Lieutenant.   "As long as we stay out of the public's sight we know we're safe."

"Safe from hostile Iranians, but what about starvation?" asked Mike.

"You're thinking too far ahead.   I think we have a better chance of finding food and water than we do surviving a run-in with Iranian militants." said Williams.

"I agree," said Lieutenant Gadsby.   "We have enough food and water for at least two days if we're sparing.   Iran isn't that big.   It can't possibly take more than a few days of walking to get back into Iraq."

"He's right," said Williams.   "The whole country of Iran is just a little bigger than the state of Texas."

Mike complained, "It takes over three days to *drive* across Texas, and yall think we can walk it in two days?"

"Actually, you can drive across Texas in one day." interrupted BB. They all looked at BB and there was a short silence between them.   BB added, "I used to drive for a trucking company in Texas."

Lieutenant Gadsby continued, "That means given my leg is broken and the type of terrain we are going through, we can estimate that it will take about three....maybe four days to walk it."

"Surely we will find water somewhere between here and there and a few days without food won't kill any of us." added Williams.

"Ok......we're following you." Mike spouted looking at Williams. "Then let's go." Williams said.

Williams started off with Mike right on his heels, followed by BB, and the Lieutenant in the rear.

General Aveev was in a meeting at the U.S. Interests Section of the Swiss Embassy in Tehran to address the issue on the growing number of US troops on the Iran/ Iraq border.   The commander of the Iranian security forces was speaking on the topic of counter objectives when General Aveev's cell phone rang.

He promptly excused himself and once in the hallway, answered after noting the caller ID, "What have you found Captain?"

Captain Ishbad said, "Sir, we have arrived at the bunker.   There was no sign of the truck anywhere along the way."

General Aveev grabbed his chin and sighed.   He looked without moving his head at the group of Public Officials and important businessmen in the room awaiting his return to continue with this pressing matter of national security.

"Prepare three trucks." he said.   "Rest your men tonight.   I'll contact you later for further instructions."   He hung up the phone without waiting for a response and pushed open the door to the conference room.

As he took his seat the President of Iran, Mahmoud Ahmadinejad said, "I trust we'll have no more interruptions."

General Aveev stood and said, "My apologies President." and sat back down.

Captain Ishbad hung the phone up and walked back up the metal stairs of the underground section of the bunker.

The largest portion of the compound was underground-------- mostly for concealment purposes.

There was only one point of access to the compound. It was protected with a top-notch surveillance system as was the entire perimeter.   Amass the eight foot tall concrete wall was over a half mile of razor-wire.

There were two roving guards.   One patrolled the north wall and the other the south wall.   They met in the middle on the east side and at the gate on the west.

The gate was guarded also by two guards.   To the right of the gate was a guard shack mainly to give the 24hr. guards a place to sit and get out of the heat occasionally.

In addition to the high-tech surveillance system and the perimeter guards there were two watchtowers.   The east tower watched for anything approaching from Birjand, Mashhad, and the Afghan border.

The west tower watched for anything coming from Semnan, Tehran, Qom, Kashan, Esfahan, Yazd, or any other bordering cities and towns. The west tower also provided more security of the gate at its base.

Inside the compound walls was a large, sturdy tent used for basic, everyday operations and maintenance.   There were at least two large transport trucks like the one that had gone missing just that morning and counting the captain's truck there was a total of eight regular trucks.

Everything on the exterior of the compound was camouflaged, in order to cloak the compound from the air.

The largest structure inside the compound was the long, three-bay building that housed all supplies, weapons, and also served as billeting to the troops that actually lived at the bunker and would rarely see anything outside the Dasht-e Kavir.

Inside the building were three levels.   The ground level which was actually about four feet below ground-level itself was the billeting area and supply warehouse.   This level was also where all vehicle maintenance was performed.

The two lower levels were strictly for weapons storage and were also heavily guarded and only accessible from to places------- the upper stairwell and the warehouse elevator.

In all, the General had around twenty or twenty-five men at his immediate disposal.   This was more than enough to keep his hidden compound very much in business.

The captain returned to the tent where he'd left his three men to wait for him.   As he approached he ordered, "Refuel the truck. Prepare two more for tomorrow.   I'll need eleven men total.   Rest tonight.

Tomorrow will be a busy day for you."

The door to the building burst open and the Corporal shouted, "Captain!" The Captain turned to look and the soldier said, "Sir, the General Sir, he's on the phone."   Captain Ishbad walked to the door and standing with his feet together leaned in and looked around.

The Corporal and two Lance Corporals were standing at attention. He entered the room and side-stepped to the right of the doorway, then snapped his fingers.   All three soldiers hurriedly vacated the room.

The captain walked to the desk and picked up the phone.   He placed it to his hear and answered, "Sir?"

The General spoke, "Tomorrow, take three trucks. Return to Kashan, then send one truck north and one south to Yazd and you go to Esfahan.   Start there and work your way back to the bunker."

"Take your time in the desert.   If there was a sand storm and the truck was already stopped it could very well have completely covered it. Captain, find that truck." Before he could speak there was a click, then a dial tone.

The captain hung the phone up and went to check on the preparation for the following day's mission.   When he entered the bay all the men snapped to attention.   The captain ignored them except for the two 1st Lieutenants he'd chosen as his best junior officers.

He informed them of the plan and told one of them to be sure and get three of the most recent area maps and put one in each truck. He turned to leave the bay and as he walked out without looking to see if his order was being obeyed he shouted, "Back to work!"

He retired to his personal quarters where he thought of the past days activities and planned for the next.   He wondered for a moment how he may have prevented this from happening at all if he'd been in charge instead of Aveeve but shook the thought from his head.   Besides, he was practically in charge anyway.

The last sliver of sun was sinking in the distance, the sand swallowing it up like the final moment before a sinking ship slips beneath the ocean waves.   Only the waves Williams had been watching for the last four hours were the heat waves of the Dasht-e Kavir.

"How're you doing back there sir?" he asked without turning to look or stopping his pace count.

"I'm still here, if that's what you're asking." replied Lieutenant Gadsby.

Williams counted 67,68,69,70, and said, "That's good enough for me." as he stopped and took a knee.

"Man it's hard to walk in this crap." fussed BB.

"Try doing it with a crutch." argued the Lieutenant.

"Look who's complaining' now!" exclaimed Mike with an, I told you so tone of voice.   "Mr. Macho ain't so macho after all huh?"

"Hey!" Williams said loudly, "Who picked your ass up about a mile back when you tripped and were cryin' like a little schoolgirl?" He looked at the Lieutenant who was pleased for some reason that the Sergeant had defended him.

Williams continued, "All right, I'm at eleven-thousand meters on my pace count so I'm guessing we've gone about six or seven miles. Does that sound right to you?" he asked looking at the Lieutenant.

The Lieutenant closed his eyes in concentration.

"Sounds right to me." said BB hoping that they were about to take a break.

"Yeah, that's about right." said the Lieutenant.

"Seven miles in four hours...... that's pretty good time, don't you think." Williams said, again looking at the Lieutenant.

BB still breathing very hard and drenched in sweat said, "I weigh two-hundred and sixty-seven pounds and it's a miracle that I'm still alive, so I say, that's damn good time. Now, can we please take a break?"

"How about, we walk for another hour or so and then stop?" Williams suggested.

"I've got an Idea." said the Lieutenant.

"What do you got?" asked Williams.

"There's a half moon out so we would be able to see each other somewhat, right?"

"Yeah." said Williams questionably.

"So, what if we spread out in a line?   As long as the fourth person keeps the other three in a straight line, theoretically, we could walk in a straight line."

"We could cover a lot more ground that way, and in the cool of the night." agreed Williams.

"Not to mention the concealment of the dark." added Lieutenant Gadsby.

Williams turned to the other two men and asked, "What do yall think?"

"Does it mean we get to take a break right now?" asked BB. Mike agreed, "Yeah, if we can stop for a few minutes I'll agree to anything."

Williams thought to himself, Mike, agree, those two words just didn't belong in the same sentence together.

"Ok then," He said, "We'll take a breather for a half hour or so and then we'll try to walk till morning." he added, almost certain he would get a protest or a grievance from someone.   He was surprised to find everyone agreeable.

Mike sat down in the sand and opened his bag.   He dug around until he found a bottle of water and twisted the cap off the plastic bottle. As he swallowed down a third of its contents in three big gulps, he reached into his jeans pocket.

He retrieved a single piece of beef jerky, still sealed in its package. He stuck the water bottle in the sand and opened the beef jerky.   He noticed Williams looking at him and pointed the jerky at him as if to offer him a piece.

"No thanks," Williams said holding his hand up at the jerky. Mike shrugged and took a bite.

BB was sprawled out in the sand, his breathing almost back to normal.

"You ok?" asked Williams as he looked down at the exhausted truck driver.

BB replied, "Yeah, I just needed to catch my breath."

"Well, make sure you drink some water, ok."

As Williams walked over to check on the Lieutenant, BB said, "Yo, Mike, toss me a bottle of that water will you?"

Mike, with a mouthful of beef jerky said, "Hold on," as he stood up and turned around to get another bottle out of his bag. "Here, catch." he said, as he tossed the bottle to BB.

"Thanks man." BB said, straining to sit up.

"How's the leg?" Williams asked as he sat down next to the Lieutenant.

"It's all right, considering." said Lieutenant Gadsby. "It's throbbing a little, but I think I'll survive."

Dragging his bag around to the front of his body, Williams said, "Here, prop your leg up on this. Maybe it'll stop the throbbing; or at least help some."

"Thanks," the Lieutenant said, leaning forward to pick his leg up and put it on the bag.

"Are you going to be able to move on that leg all night." asked Williams.

"I don't see where I have a choice." replied the Lieutenant. "Besides, the sooner we get back the sooner I can get the medical attention that I need. I may be a paper pusher but I know when I have to be tough and when I can bathe in self-pity. This is one of those times that I have to be strong."

"How about that scratch on your back?" he asked sarcastically.

"Oh it's fine," Williams said, nonchalantly.

The Lieutenant looked at him skeptically and said, "I may be gullible but I'm not stupid and that's too much blood to be *just a scratch*." He gave a gesture with his crutch at the crimson stain on Williams' shirt-tail.

Williams looked at the Lieutenant whose face was suggesting that he wanted an answer; not an excuse. He could feel the sharp pain in his lower back that he'd been fighting perpetually to ignore since they'd left the crash site.

Reluctantly, he said, "I think I've got a piece of shrapnel from the plane stuck in there. Every time I move a certain way I can feel it."

"Do you think we need to try and remove it?" the Lieutenant asked.

"No it's in there pretty deep, and I'm afraid it would bleed worse if you tried to dig it out."

"What if it gets infected?" he asked looking at his leg wondering the same thing about his own wounds. He hoped that the Sergeants answer would help him decide how to feel about his own leg.

Williams shrugged and said, "I guess that's a risk I'm going to have to take."

He didn't particularly like the answer that he got but he didn't have a better one so he just said, "Me too Sergeant, me too."

For the next half hour they sat and attempted to enjoy the quiet tranquility when Williams said, "We should probably get going while we still have the temperature on our side."

The Lieutenant climbed to his feet and agreed, "Your right, "We can rest more during the day when it is too hot to be marching through this Godforsaken desert."

Reluctantly Mike and BB staggered to their feet and threw their bags onto their backs. Mike had been almost asleep when BB nudged him awake so he really didn't know whether they'd been there for a half an hour or half the night.

As Williams walked past him he grinned and asked, "What, no

argument?" Mike sneered at him with resentment but remained silent. He was learning fast that most of his comments just caused more conflict and he was too tired to argue.

"Remember the line formation that we talked about earlier?" asked Williams.   Everyone nodded including Mike, who did so while rubbing his eye with his one good arm.

"Good, then let's go." he said as he trudged forward through the thick sand.   BB followed with Mike in tow, and the Lieutenant picked up the rear saying, "Spread it out some Mike."

Mike rolled his eyes as he stopped, dead in his tracks allowing BB to put some distance between them before resuming his forward plodding through the loosely packed sand beneath his feet.

All night they walked occasionally taking a break to drink some water, let BB catch his breath, or to take record of the distance they'd traveled.

It was getting light now and the terrain was beginning to change. The vast open desert was becoming more rugged, and more burdensome to traverse.

The previous day they could see for miles in all directions.   Now their vision was restricted amply by the rocky manacles that surrounded them like a maze of stone.

They huddled together to discuss how to tackle this new obstacle. "This is definitely going to complicate things for us.   Not only is it going to be much more difficult for you to get through the rougher terrain," Williams said, giving a nod in the Lieutenants' direction.   "It's also going to be a lot harder to keep on a straight path at night."

"Are you suggesting we keep walking all day now?" Mike asked. "You do realize we just walked all night don't you?"

"Of course I do, but that doesn't change the fact that we are going to have allot more difficulty making good time through this type of terrain." Williams argued.

The Lieutenant spoke up. "What about half and half?   I say, we sleep until noon or so and then hike until midnight.   That way, if we do get a little of course traveling in the dark we will only have gone half as far and can get back on track during the morning after."

"I'm cool with that," BB said, and looked at Mike. Mike admitted, "That sounds better than walking all day."

Williams said, "The sun isn't all the way up yet.   Are there any objections to going a little farther before it gets too hot and then sleeping a little later than twelve?"

He looked at Lieutenant Gadsby as if it were his decision, ultimately.   "I think I could manage another mile or two." he said with shaky confidence.

Williams shifted his regard to Mike and BB.   BB gave a lackadaisical shrug as Mike said, "I don't care, whatever."   As he threw his bag back on and turned his back to the group, he muttered, "It don't matter what I think anyway."

They navigated through the trivial new terrain, up hills and rocky pinnacles, and in and out through the rocky maze.

As Williams clawed his way to the top of a ridge he almost trampled BB as he scurried back down almost in a panic.

He motioned for every ones attention as if to make no noise if possible.   They huddled together and pointing up at his point of retreat, Williams whispered, "There is some sort of little camp or village about fifty meters over that ridge."

"Does it look like militia or anything hostile?" asked the Lieutenant.

"I don't know.   I didn't get that good of a look.   I'll check it out. You all just keep your eyes open for anything suspicious."

He climbed back to the top of the ridge as stealthily as he could and peered over the top.   He squinted to see.   The hair on his neck was standing up and his knees began to quiver but not so much that it was noticeable.

He drew a mental map as best he could of the tiny little camp. There was one small, but permanent building that looked to be built of adobe type bricks.   There was a small open-wall shed that looked like it was used as a stable of sort.

There was a small wagon next to the building and just beyond the wagon was a phone booth sized shack that he assumed was an outhouse. On the east side of the stable was a makeshift corral that contained one, somewhat, pitiful looking donkey.

Just as he was about to return and report his recordings a short, well-dressed man emerged from the building. He walked out to the stable where he was met by a local Arabic man. After a short conversation the Arabic man returned to his work, whatever it had been, and the well-dressed man back the building he originated from.

As the man returned to the building Williams strained his eyes to get a better look. -----*Could it be... is... he... was he...an American!*   The man vanished back into the building and Williams returned to his faction of MIA's

"They don't look hostile." he said squatting beside the already huddled trio.

"Yeah, but those kids they send through our checkpoints with bombs strapped to them don't look hostile either do they?" asked the Lieutenant.

"There's something else." Williams said.

"What?" asked Mike.

"There's a.... an American down there."

"An American!" exclaimed Mike. "Then what are we waiting for? Let's go down there."

"Slow down there, wild man." interrupted Williams simultaneously grabbing Mike by his shirt and pulling him back to a squat. "Just because he's American doesn't make him friendly. He doesn't look like a threat, but like the Lieutenant said, you never can tell in this place."

"So, what do we do?" asked BB.

While unslinging his rifle and handing it to Mike, Williams said, "I'll go down and check things out.   Ya'll cover me just in case."

"You're going down there unarmed?" asked Mike in disbelief.

"Of course I'm not." Williams said, as he drew the 9mm from his waistband.   He chambered the first round and said, "Here I go."

"Be careful." cautioned the Lieutenant.

Williams checked that the coast was clear and started down the embankment holding the 9mm low as to conceal it.   He didn't want to provoke an otherwise peaceful stranger.

CHAPTER 4

"THE DOCTOR"

Williams approached the small brick building with caution and carefully announced his presence. "Hello." he said stepping through the already opened doorway, his right hand still firmly gripping the 9mm as he tucked it back into his waistband.

He wondered if he should have kept it at the ready but voted to keep it concealed for now. The little building had had an additional wall built to divide the already tiny room into two separate rooms. The first room was unoccupied therefore he assumed that the man they'd seen must be in the next one.

"Hello," he announced again, this time answered by a very American accent. "One moment. Anna didn't say she was bringing......" The man froze as he examined the uniformed stranger standing in his office doorway, and although stunned finished his sentence with, "friends with her."

The man was considerably aged and was drying his hands with a clean white hand towel so Williams judged him not to be a threat.

He raised his hands to show he meant no harm and said, "I am a friend, but I'm afraid I don't know Anna sir."

The man judged Williams also non-threatening and stepped forward placing the hand towel on the table beside the door he'd entered the room through.   "What is your business here then?" the man asked.

"Sir, My name is Keith Williams.   I am an American Soldier.   I was deployed to Iraq and I was on my way home for leave when my plane went down about twenty miles east of here.   I have three more men accompanying me.   We've been walking all night sir and we're tired, lost and two..." he paused thinking about his conversation with the Lieutenant the night before, "Well, three of us are injured from the crash."

The man sighed and said, "Get your men and bring them to the large tent directly behind this building."

Williams asked, "The locals here, will they be alarmed?"

"I will take care of that." the gentleman said as he stepped outside and shouted something in Arabic.

A young Arabic man came to him and gave Williams a double take. The American man said something else in the Arabic dialect.   The man said something back to him and walked away as if everything was normal.

He turned to Williams and said, "It's ok, go fetch your friends."

Williams walked out of the building and looked up into the rocks where his fellow travelers were eagerly awaiting his approval. He motioned for them to come down.   The man looked with a squint toward the rocks where Williams had motioned and three heads appeared from the scraggy hillside.

As they walked toward the tent Williams asked the man," Do you mind if I ask what an American like yourself is doing here?"

He answered, "Well I certainly didn't fall out of the sky as you did."   He looked over his shoulder for a reaction but none of them found it funny.

He continued, "My name is Robert Herren I was a practicing Family Doctor in Arkansas for thirty-six years.   When I retired I wanted to help less fortunate people in these impoverished countries.   The Red Cross didn't agree with me on my ideals and desires to reach out beyond the safety of their camps, so I began working independently."

"For three years I have followed these herdsmen and provided them with medical care that their country cannot or will not provide for them."

"However, I am getting old and cannot travel like I used to so they come to me as their herds pass through this part of the desert.   This is my home."

As the doctor pushed open the canvas door of the tent he said, "And this is my clinic. It's not much for a clinic but it gets the job done." He unbuttoned his sleeves and removed a large plastic cover from over an old but clean examination table and said, "You there, with the leg. Go ahead and take your splint off."

The tent was surprisingly spacious.   Williams guessed it was British, maybe French made.   He thought how it looked like a scene from Indiana Jones.   The walls were lined with large wooden crates except for the back wall and the right front corner.

The entire back wall was filled with medical equipment and cabinets.   All of which were covered with plastic sheeting except for the cabinet directly behind the table because the doctor had just removed it also.

In the front corner, to the immediate right of the entrance there were no crates, but it wasn't empty.   There was a small bed that should probably have been classified as a cot.   In the very corner was a tiny table stand adorned by a small cloth and some sort of statuette and a candle.

The Lieutenant limped to the table where Williams assisted him in the removal of his improvised splint.   "Careful," said Lieutenant Gadsby, grimacing with the pain that was increasing with intensity as the circulation was restored with the loosening of the splint.

The doctor was rolling up his sleeves now and rattling around in his medical cabinet.   "How long have you been traveling?" he asked, as he snapped a latex glove onto his right hand.

Williams answered, "About a half day and one full night."

"You must be ravished?" he remarked, snapping the second glove on his left hand.

"Starving!" bellowed BB who was sitting on a crate next to the door.

"I'll see what I can do for you here shortly." said the doctor while cutting the Lieutenants pant leg.

The doctor cleaned the wounds on the Lieutenants leg and applied a more suitable splint on it.   He said, "This splint will allow for the maximum movement considering you'll need to be mobile."

"Do you have anything as far as pain relievers?"

The doctor turned and looked at his cabinet.   He walked to it and when he found what he was looking for said, "Ahh there you are."   He took a bottle from the shelf and returned to the table.   He handed the bottle to the Lieutenant and said, "It's not prescription but it should help a bit."

After he finished with the Lieutenant he asked, "Who's next?" Mike walked over to the table.   The doctor asked, "Who made this splint?"

Mike pointed at Sergeant Williams with his good arm.   "He did."

The doctor looked at Williams and said, "You did good sir."

"Thanks," Williams said as he shook the dust off of a crutch he'd found propped in the corner next to several more crates, these marked with the Red Cross logo.

"Do you have two of these?" he asked holding the crutch up for the doctor to see.

"Behind the casket."   He suggested nodding at a tall wooden box in the corner behind BB.   They all gave the doctor a moot look. The doctor, taking note of their demeanor said, "You can't save them all."

BB was falling asleep on his crate and was starting to snore. Williams looked at the Lieutenant who smiled in agreement that it was a little humorous.

The doctor rewrapped Mike's arm and scanned the remaining two men saying, "I thought you said three of you were hurt?"

Williams removed his shirt and pulled the 9mm from his belt. He placed it on the table opposite the doctor but still very much within reach.

The doctor glanced at the pistol as he lifted the back of Williams' shirt.   "I prefer to keep it close."   Williams said, noticing the doctors' glance.

"I understand," replied the doctor, "but you are safe here."

"However," he continued, "You are smart for avoiding heavily populated areas.   The local Iranian people are typically uneducated and do not understand the political issues that their leaders are struggling with and at times fight about."

"Iran's government is in shambles and the heads of government in this country spend more time fighting over their beliefs than working to resolve issues pertaining to the people.   Due to the local peoples philistinism they believe that the American people just want to take over like they did in Iraq."

"We are trying to help in Iraq not take over Iraq." argued Mike.

"Yes *I know this.*   The problem is the local people do not know what a democracy, or any form of organized government is for that matter.   Therefore, they don't understand that America is actually trying to help.

"What do they think we want to take over?"   Mike spouted. "There's nothing here but sand, sand, and more damn sand!   If I were them I'd be trying to hitch a ride out of this dump.   What kind of idiot want's to live here anyway?"   He looked at the doctor and added, "No offense."

"None taken."   The doctor said with a smile.

"I'm going to need you to lay down for me." he told Williams.   He lay down on the table and the doctor said," This may hurt a bit." as he took a pair of scissor-clamps and repositioned his work light.   He leaned over the Sergeant to get a closer look.

Williams tensed up in preparation for what he knew would be quite painful.   The doctor held open the laceration and surprisingly with great ease of effort removed a small piece of metallic material. He gave it a quick look and dropped it into a small metal tray about two inches deep and half full of some clear solution that turned to a dark red when the bloody shard was dropped into it.

Williams immediately felt relieved and then pain as the doctor poured alcohol over the wound to flush out any traces of infection. He thought he might yell in pain but clenched his teeth so not to show weakness in front of his newfound friends.

The doctor then began preparing a large curved needle and surgical thread.   Williams said, "Is there any chance you could numb it up some first?"

"Sorry," replied the doctor.   "Anesthetics are a luxury we don't possess here in the desert."

Williams asked with a flinch, "Why.....don't the locals have a problem wi.......th you?"

The doctor answered as he wiped away some blood from where he was working, "First of all, where we are right now there are no locals. Secondly, if there were they don't usually give medical personnel any grief."

"Two US uniforms probably wouldn't fare too well in a considerably populated area.   Not to mention your carrying two rifles and a rocket launcher, or whatever that thing is."   He pointed to the RPG tube propped against the wall of the tent next to BB who was head bobbing and swaying back and forth.

After he'd finished stitching him up and properly bandaging him the doctor said, "You are very fortunate that the debris didn't puncture anything internally."   Williams sat up and for a minute thought that he might pass out but after a few deep breaths was clear-headed again.

"What about that food Doc?"   BB asked after the wind slapped the door of the tent against the wall and woke him.

"Yes, of course.   Come with me," the doctor said.   Williams handed the Lieutenant the crutches and they followed the doctor back outside.

Lieutenant Gadsby asked, "Did you get a good nap BB?" Williams snorted a laugh.

"I can't help I'm tired man."   BB argued in his own defense.

"I know. I'm just picking on you." said the Lieutenant.   BB grinned and followed him out.

Outside the tent and to the left was a small container box used for shipping cargo by railroad and container ships.   The doctor opened the box which wasn't locked or secured in anyway other than the latch used to secure the door.

Inside the box were additional medical supplies and some more crates with the Red Cross logo on them.   He opened one of the crates and gathered a handful of prepackaged non-perishable meals; much like the MRE's that they still had a few of in the bag that Williams had carried.

As they walked back out into the yard the doctor said, "I wish that I could help you more but I have no transportation and the nearest city is Kashan, which is northwest of here, or Esfahan which is southwest, both of which are some one-hundred and sixty kilometers from here.   That's about one-hundred miles."

"There's a city southwest of here?"   Williams questioned.

"Yes. Esfahan." the doctor replied.

BB opened his packaged meal, and asked, "Weren't we trying to stay away from the cities?"

"Yes," explained Williams.   "We are trying to get back to the Iraqi border without running into too much civilization."

The doctor smiled and said, "That is possible but I think I may know a better way for you to get back to where you need to go. There is a Red Cross camp eighty kilometers from here.   That's right at fifty miles.   It's in the direction you were going but a little more west than south."

Williams noticed the man working at the little makeshift stable. "Who's he?" he asked.

"That's Ali Habbin," the doctor answered. "He keeps the place up and mostly takes care of my ass."   BB stopped dead in his tracks and looked at the Lieutenant wide-eyed.

The Lieutenant chuckled and whispered, "Donkey."

"Oh!"   BB whispered back as he resumed chewing.

78

The doctor said "You're welcome to rest here as long as you like. I don't have much room but I have plenty of food and clean water, no running water but clean water.   The toilet is around back and Al will cook dinner for us around five."

After dinner they sat on crates in front of the doctor's house discussing their plans for the following day.   Williams said, "I guess tomorrow we will leave for the Red Cross camp."

The doctor was standing in the doorway of the little building and said, "I wish you had come later in the month.   My niece is at the Red Cross camp as we speak and is going to be coming to visit me."

"When?" asked Williams.

"She could be here tomorrow or two weeks from now.   It just depends on how busy she is at the orphanage."

"Orphanage?" asked Williams.

"Yes, there is a small orphanage at the camp, eight or ten kids, that's all.   Anna likes to visit the children at least twice a year.   It's probably because she was an orphan herself.   My brother Roger and his wife Alanna were killed when she was nine during a rebel attack on an African village where they were a part of the relief effort.   They would be so proud of her now."

"She is a pediatrician back in the US.   She comes to see the children but I like to think she comes just for me." the doctor said, and smiled as he leaned against the door jamb of the little house.

Williams thought aloud, "50 miles, 4 per hour, 40 in 10hours." "I could do it." he said.

"Do what?" asked the Lieutenant already knowing what he had in mind.

"I could make the camp in less than two days and come back with the doctors' niece for the rest of you."

"You can't go alone.   Someone will need to go with you." said the Lieutenant.

"Why?" asked Williams.

"It's just better to at least be split into pairs, rather than running across the desert alone."

"Don't look at me." said Mike.

BB protested, "You think I can make it better than you?"

"As a matter of fact I do.   He's talking about running.   I have asthma.   It was hard enough to walk the other night."

They all gave him a questionable look.

"Honest to God I do!   I always have!" he pleaded.

Williams turned and looked at BB.   BB had his eyes shut shaking his head as he said, "I knew I shoulda' went on a damn diet." He opened his eyes and asked, "When do we leave?"

"You sure you can do this?"   Williams asked.

"I played ball in school and it's been a while but I know if I want it bad enough I can."

"How about lunchtime tomorrow?" asked Williams.

"I'm goin to sleep.   You just get me when you get ready to go." BB said as he climbed onto the wagon beside the little brick house.

"I think I will turn in also." said Williams and strolled away to find a good place lay down.   Mike and the Lieutenant soon followed Williams to the tent where Ali was also preparing for bed.   He smiled and in very bad English bid them goodnight.   They each found themselves a suitable place and after a short time it was quiet.

It was daylight now and the Captain and his men had been searching all night with no luck.   It was time to report to the General, and the Captain had nothing to show after almost twenty-four hours of continuous searching.   The General was not going to be happy.

Captain Ishbad took out his cell phone and dialed.

"Hello, sir I have searched Esfahan and the first truck has returned from Qom.   My third team just reported that they also have seen nothing.

The General replied, "Intensify your search.   Go out to the

81

smaller surrounding villages and if need be start questioning people I don't care what it takes.   I will meet you in Kashan this evening at the warehouse.   We must find that shipment.   Is this clear Captain?"

"Yes Sir." answered Captain Ishbad.

As he hung up the phone his third truck arrived with some new information.   They had gotten word of an American doctor that lived in the desert and provided medical attention to the traveling herdsmen.

"The doctor's house is located only a few kilometers south of the route we take through the Dasht e Kavir to get to the Bunker." said the Lieutenant.

The Captain thought to himself, if the truck had been caught in the sandstorm they may have gotten disoriented and wavered from their regular course.   There was a good chance that if this was true, and they had been stranded, the doctor may have seen them.

He was tired and his men were tired but he couldn't afford to sleep when he might be on to something.   He must go to the doctor. The General was getting impatient and Captain Ishbad could not...he would not let him down.

He ordered his men to load up.   They were going to the doctor. He was sure to know something.   If he didn't, he knew the local herdsmen and they would possibly have told him if they'd seen anything out of the ordinary.

It'd been too long; she thought as Anna folded a shirt and put it on top of her favorite pair of blue jeans.   She joked about them once with a friend, saying that they were her lucky jeans.   She double checked that she had packed all the necessary items for four days in the desert.

She was only planning on staying for three but she had always made it a habit to pack an extra days' worth of everything all the way down to the socks.   She would always say, "Better to go overboard than under-prepared."

Anna was thirty years old and had been a pediatric doctor in Little Rock AS for two years.   She had a passion for working with children and had for as long as she could remember.   A trait, she thought, was most likely picked up from her mother.

As she closed her suitcase, still deep in thought, she was startled by a knock on the door.   "It's open!" she proclaimed, as she zipped the suitcase shut.   She had to re-zip the left side twice.   It had been broken for almost a year and she had just not had the time to buy a new suitcase.

"Miss Herren," the voice came from the door of her small, but comfortable room.

"Good morning Nurse Bennett.   How are you today?"

"I'm well, thank you.   Have you seen Tamillee?   She's not in the orphanage."

"No, she's not here.   Did you check the garden?   She likes to draw pictures of the flowers there."   Anna pushed the drawer of the dresser shut as she took her brush from under a pile of papers. "Can't leave without this now can I?" she asked jovially.

"That would be devastating." said Nurse Bennett with a smile. "I will check the garden."

As she began to pull the door too Anna asked, "Oh, Nurse Bennett, could you send her here when you find her?"

"Sure thing Miss Herren." she said as she closed the door.

Tamillee was 11 years old.   Her mother had been arrested for taking part in a Pro-democracy demonstration in Tehran during the late 90's.   She was denied a fair trial and sentenced to death by a Revolutionary Court in August of 1999.

Tamillee's father, three years later was murdered during a similar demonstration in Karaj by Basiji forces.   The Basiji, referred to as the "plainclothes" was basically an anti-demonstrator organization thrown together by the Iranian government in 2002.

She had spent the last five years of her life at the Red Cross orphanage and had become one of Anna's favorites. Anna had actually come bearing good news for Tamillee this year. She had found a foster home for her and couldn't wait to tell her about it.

Tamillee wanted to be an artist and was actually quite talented. She would spend hours every day in the garden greenhouse drawing pictures of the flowers there. Due to her love for flowers and the hours she spent drawing them in the greenhouse, Tamillee had earned the nickname "flower girl" and it fit her fine.

She had drawn Snowflake flowers, Crown Imperials, and Crocus flowers. She was just finishing a drawing of Saffron, a flower that grows all across the Middle East and is commonly used as a type of spice when Nurse Bennett appeared in the doorway of the tiny greenhouse.

"Good morning Tami." said Nurse Bennett, as she approached her. "I believe someone is looking for you."

"Miss Anna?" she asked. Tamillee had been waiting all morning. She knew that Anna would want to see her soon.
She closed her sketchpad and stuck her pencils into her pocket.

"She asked me to send you to see her. You must not keep her waiting." said Nurse Bennett as she pushed open the screen door behind her for Tamillee to walk through.

Tamillee scurried past the cordial nurse and through the courtyard. As she made her way to Anna's room she disrupted a drove of chickens. They were pecking at the ground in hopes that they may actually find some hint of a scrap missed by the others.

It took less than 30 seconds to make the trip from the greenhouse to the guest pod.   It was a considerably small camp and the only reason that the organization had kept it open was because of its convenient location next to the railroad tracks.

The camp had been there for years, six to be exact.   Because of its remote location it was difficult to get the more important supplies to them in a considerable amount of time and this kept the camp from being funded anything over its annual budgeted amount.

The facilities were becoming run down and their equipment was outdated.   Like most every village or small town in Iran there were very few structurally sound buildings in the camp.   In fact if you counted the greenhouse there were only four.

There was the main clinic that would facilitate *comfortably,* about six patients and that was stretching it.   The only other block buildings were the orphanage and the ten room housing pod where the doctors and nurses had personal rooms and the teacher had claimed one of the remaining guest rooms that were usually a little larger and shared by temps.   All rooms were divided by a central, shared bathroom with a shower and sink.   There was still no sewage so the whole site shared a centralized four stall portable toilet with a large holding tank that was emptied monthly by a local waste management company.   (Local being an understatement)

There was a skeleton faculty that ran the camp.   The camp had two doctors, four nurses, and usually four to six volunteer, temps. Just the last year, they had added a teacher to start teaching the children. She educated them on the basic reading and writing skills and taught them the English language.   Many of the children would be adopted by American families just as Tamillee, and knowing the English language would be very helpful in their adaption to culture change.

As Tami approached Anna's door she tucked her loose, jet black hair behind her ears and tapped on the door.   The door opened almost immediately and Anna exclaimed, "Tami!" as she knelt to get a hug.

"How are you doing with your school work?"   Anna asked.

"Fine; I need to improve my reading and writing in English but everything else is good." she replied as she plopped herself on the edge of the low cut single bed.

"Your spoken English is definitely doing well I see.   You could hardly carry a conversation when I left last year."

"I've been doing my studies, and reading your letters helps me with my English."

"Your teacher told me that you were ahead of all the students in the camp.   She said that since you were so far ahead that you can go with me to visit my uncle in the desert.   How does that sound too you?"

She was so excited that all she could do is grin and bounce up and down excitedly.

"Well, are you packed yet?"   We are leaving in about an hour.

"I will, right now!"   Tami said as she ran away to the orphanage.

Outside at the rental van she met Doctor Javier who was always pleased to see Anna.   "Hello doctor." she said as she fought the bulky case into the back of the van.

"Can I assist you with that?" he asked.

"I think I got it, but thank you anyway." she replied hoping he would leave her alone and go back to his harassing one of the other nurses.

Doctor Javier was the only part of visiting that Anna always dreaded.   He followed her around like a dog in heat every time she came and she had tried everything to get him to leave her alone.

She had threatened to bring her boyfriend with her which was just a bluff because she hadn't had a significant relationship with anyone in the last four years.   At least not since her last boy-friend dumped her due to her being "too busy with her work."

She had made it known that he was old enough to be her father and still Doctor Javier didn't get it, or just didn't care rather.   She was relieved to be leaving for a few days and wouldn't have to deal with him until she returned.

She was used to being flirted with. She was considerably attractive with shoulder length, auburn hair, deep blue eyes and a near perfect complexion. She weighed 120lbs soaking wet and like most women thought she was fat. She was often the center of attention, especially when in the company of men. Her uncle always wondered why she was always single when she came to visit and would ask her when she was going to find someone to settle down with but she had no desire to settle down. Her focus was on her career as a young doctor and she had little time for social life.

Nurse Bennett and Tamillee came to her rescue and put Doctor Javier to work loading Tamillee's bags and supplies for their trip.

"We will be leaving right after lunch. Are you ready Tami?" Anna asked as she walked to the passenger door of the van and opened it to retrieve a rectangular package wrapped in shiny red paper.

Tamillee nodded as she handed Doctor Javier her small duffel bag. Much like the bag Anna used back home as her gym bag she thought.

"I brought you a gift for your birthday." Anna said handing the package to her.

As she took it Tamillee said, "But it's not my birthday yet."

"I know but I thought you could use it early." she answered smiling.

Tamillee tore the paper off the box and excitedly dropping the paper on the ground where Nurse Bennett instinctively picked it up. She then opened the box to find a small wooden case with a single latch and a small carrying handle.   Anna took the box from her and handed it to the nurse.

Tami opened the case to reveal a complete set of color-pencils and metal-bound sketchpad.   "It even has a sharpener." Anna said pointing to the little handheld pencil sharpener in its own slot inside the case.

Tami closed the case and wrapped her arms around Anna. "Thank you, thank you, thank you, she said with her face buried in Anna's shoulder.

"You're welcome."   Anna said, not surprised at Tami's reaction but still touched and fighting back tears added, "I knew you could put them to good use."

"I will," she said with a smile that made Anna's day, and she hadn't even given her the best news yet.

"You'll have to draw Nurse Bennett a picture of something on our trip."

"I would like that very much." said Nurse Bennett still smiling also.

"I will.   I will draw her a picture of your uncle."

"That would be nice." said Nurse Bennett.

CHAPTER 5

"THE REALIZATION"

Williams and the Lieutenant woke BB and told him it was time.

"Ok BB," said Williams, "Until dark we will just walk at a fast pace to conserve energy for tonight.   Once it gets dark we will pick up the pace for as far as we can.   Then after a short break, we'll do it again."

"Ok," he said rubbing his eyes.

"I have as much water as I can carry in our bags and I only put one MRE apiece in because we need to travel as light as we can, and still have enough water."

"What time is it?" he asked.

"It's nine in the morning but the sooner we leave the better."

Within the next half hour they were on their way, BB with the Lieutenant's 9mm and Williams with the other 9mm and an AK-47. The doctor pointed them in the right direction and wished them luck.

As they walked BB said, "If I ever want to hide something I know where I'll hide it."

"Where's that?" asked Williams.

"Here!" he exclaimed.   "We ain't been half a mile yet and I couldn't find my way back if somebody was shooting at me."

Williams laughed.   "Makes you wonder how those herdsmen find their way around out here doesn't it?"

"Even those three wise men in the bible got a star to follow.   I guess even God thought we didn't have no business out here without something to follow.   You know what I'm sayin' Sarge?"

Already laughing he agreed, "Yeah BB, I definitely agree with that one."

BB wrinkled his forehead in thought and asked, "Are you really wanting to run when it gets dark, cause I don't really know how long my big ass can keep up a full run?"

"Maybe not a full run BB, but we're gonna have to huff it. Maybe a quick jog, you know?"   Williams replied.

"Just don't run off and leave me out here, aight."

"Don't worry........."

A single crack echoed in the distance.   They both froze.   Then, another two, *Gunshots!*   "What the hell!" exclaimed BB.

"Shhh, get down!"   Williams said quietly but with fervor.

"You think they're tryin' to get our attention?"   BB asked.

"No," Williams said, "They know we would have heard just one shot.

They wouldn't have risked making that much noise.   Besides, I'm no expert but that sounded like a pistol, and we've got both of ours."

"C-mon." he said, as he headed back towards the doctors. This time he was almost running and BB was having a hard time keeping up with him.

Once they got close, Williams stopped and walked, staying low and trying not to make any noise if at all possible.   He found himself back in the same situation he was just in a day earlier, only this time, even scarier.

He crawled to the top of the ridge and immediately saw what he feared most.   There were three Iranian militants.   Two were carrying the lifeless bodies of Ali, the Doctor, and Lieutenant Gadsby into the little building.   The other was standing in the middle of the driveway pacing as if he were keeping a lookout for something.

He slowly slid back down to BB.   He was panting, and not just trying to catch his breath.   Williams found himself fighting back panic once again.   Trying not to hyperventilate, he slowed his breathing, took a few deep breaths and said, "Ok."

"Ok what?" asked BB worriedly.

"We're in big trouble BB.

"Why?"

"I didn't see Mike, but I'm pretty certain that the doctor, Lieutenant Gadsby, and Ali are dead."

"Dead?" BB asked in disbelief, and began to panic a little himself.

"There are at least, three guys down there, and they look like Iranian military or something.   They are obviously armed and hostile. I don't know if they already took Mikes body into the house or if he's down there hiding somewhere.   If he is, it won't be long before they find him, and we both have a good idea what will happen then."

"I have to go down there and take them out, and I am going to need your help."

"Are you crazy?"   BB pleaded.

"BB, we don't have time to argue.   Are you with me, or not?"

BB closed his eyes in thought, wrinkled his forehead again, slowed his breathing, and said, "What do you need me to do?"

"Follow me."   Williams said as he worked his way around to the east, and then the north side of the property.   Quickly, and carefully, they made their way through the rocky terrain until they made it to the north east side, almost where they'd been the day before.

Williams asked, "Do you know how to shoot that AK?"

"Yeah, the Lieutenant showed me last night."   BB replied.

"When I go, you follow, unless I say stop, and all you do is point and shoot if I say to.   Otherwise, just be quiet, and stay out of sight."

"Ok."   BB whispered, as he collected his thoughts, and again took a deep breath.

Before he knew it Williams was gone, scurrying down the hill like a bat outta hell, pistol at the ready.   He jumped to his feet and followed in suit.

Williams stopped at the outhouse and waited for BB to catch up, "You stay here, but watch me.   I'll tell you where to go.   Remember, only shoot if I'm dead, or tell you to."

"What if they see me?"   BB asked quietly.

"Then I'm dead."   Williams said as he turned and darted for the back corner of the house.

Williams made his way down the side of the house keeping close to the windowless brick wall.   When he reached the corner he thought to himself, *there are three of them.   I can handle two easy but I need to get one quietly.*   He remembered the knife in his pocket.

He reached into his pocket slowly to retrieve the knife.   It was about nine inches long opened, and plenty long enough for the job Williams thought. He knelt slowly to open the knife and then, *"Oh my God, he's right there... just inches from me."*

He looked up to see where the soldiers face was turned.   It was turned away.   He peeked around the corner to see where the other two were.   The one was still in the driveway and he couldn't get eyes on the third one.

He was terrified, but the adrenaline took over.   He stood slowly keeping his eyes on the man's head to ensure his back stayed turned. He leaned out, enough to see where the other man was looking.   He had his back turned.

It was now or never.
He couldn't wait, it had to be now.
All sound vanished.   It was as if it were just him, and his target. He could smell the man's body odor.   He stepped forward, looked, no sign of the third guy.   The one in the driveway still had his back turned.

Both hands.......

One motion......

Left hand over the mouth, and right hand with the knife..........

He sunk the blade all the way, with all his might, in one side and out the other side of the man's throat.
He immediately dragged him backward and out of sight around the corner.   The man was shaking and thrashing wildly.   Williams without looking at the man's face watched the corner of the house and gave the knife a quick twist.   There was blood everywhere and after just seconds the man was still.

Williams stood.   He turned to BB who was wide-eyed and staring in disbelief.

He motioned with two fingers in a swift wave, for him to move to the backside of the house.   BB moved to the corner, knelt as he had seen Williams do, and waited.

Williams left the knife and picked up the 9mm.   He returned to the corner where he was surprised to find the guy in the driveway completely oblivious to what had just happened.   He laid down the 9mm and picked up the dead soldiers AK-47.

He didn't know if the third guy was in the house or not but if he was he had to come out the door and wouldn't stand a chance against an automatic weapon.   Once again he took a deep breath worked up his courage and stepped out from around the corner.

The guy in the driveway never knew what hit him he was down in less than a second.   Williams turned to the door of the house and waited for the third guy to come rushing out.

Nothing...........

No-one rushed out.

He worked up the courage to kick the door open.

Apparently it took the third guy the same amount of time to get up the courage to come out of the cargo box at the back side of the camp because as Williams kicked the door in he saw him run out in the corner of his eye.

He turned and fired as he continued forward into the house. He yelled, "Shoot BB, shoot, shoot, shoot! Williams fired back and one of the third man's rounds found its mark on the upper right shoulder of Williams spinning him backward and to the floor.

Silence swept over the whole place. Then BB stepped out. The third man had been hit by one of their rounds and it didn't matter whose it was, as long as he was down. "BB?" came Williams' voice from the little house.

"Oh, Thank the Lord, I thought you were dead." BB said with relief.

"I probably would be if you hadn't opened up on him. What was the hold up?"

"I didn't.......You said not to shoot unless you said to."

"Well, you could've been a little quicker." He looked at his shoulder which was bleeding a little by this time. "Come give me a hand with this." he said as he walked toward the tent.

They entered the tent and Williams walked to the table where he laid the rifle down and took his shirt off. "I think it's a clean shot." he said. BB looked at his shoulder and said, "Yeah." He pointed as he

98

said, "It looks like it just went in there and out the back."

"I'm going to need some gauze and something to wrap around it."

BB brought the requested items and asked, "What do want me to do?"

"Just wrap it while I hold the gauze."   Williams said while holding the gauze in place and scoffing at the pain.   BB wrapped the bandage tight around the gauze and under Williams' other arm. When he was done he helped him with his shirt and asked, "What do we do now?"

There was a sound in the corner.   They both jumped with surprise.   Williams grabbed the 9mm and held his bad arm out in front of BB as to tell him to back up.   As he approached the small wooden box he called out, "Mike!"   He stepped closer.   "Is that you Mike?"   The lid to the casket came open as Mike stepped out.

"Shit Mike!"   Williams exclaimed.   "I almost shot you dead! Why didn't you come outta there when you heard us in here?"

"I was scared." said Mike, pale faced and still shaking all over.

"You're ok now Mike come on over here and let's figure out what we're gonna do now."   Williams said, motioning with the 9mm because he had just realized that he could hardly feel his right arm. Mike walked over to them and quietly said, "I need some more pants."   BB almost laughed, thinking it was a joke, but realized that Mike was dead serious.

Williams realizing what had happened said softly, "It's ok man. Come sit down and we'll see what we can do for you."   He motioned for

BB to go outside and told Mike he'd be right back.

Outside the tent Williams said, "BB, see if you can find something clean for him and don't talk about it.   He's pretty traumatized and this kind of thing can really be bad."   BB said, "I gotcha.   I'll see what I can find."

Williams went back to Mike and said, "Mike, I know you were scared and it's ok.   I was scared too, but I need to know if you saw or heard anything that may help us figure out what just happened. Do you think you can do that for me?"

Mike said, "I'm not losing it.   You don't have to talk all slow for me I just had to go and that son-of-a-bitch almost found me.   I think he saw the RPG thing and that's why he didn't find me."

Williams looked to the corner where they had left the extra weapons.   They were gone.   He asked, "Could you hear anything or see anything?"

"I heard the Lieutenant say something about another American soldier, the Red Cross, and the plane crash.   Everything seemed to be going good until that little sucker found the weapons.   After that, the Iranian guy started yelling and then it got quiet.   I thought maybe they had left but when I started to get out and check that's when........"

"It's all right.   I got the rest."   Williams said.   BB came through the door announcing, "Don't shoot, it's just me.   I found these but they're gonna be a little big on ya."

"They'll work.   Thanks BB."   Mike said.

"No problem."   BB answered.

"Hey BB, about that...... you know, don't tell..."

BB interrupted, "Don't worry bout that.   I done already forgot about it."   He smiled.

Mike smiled back and said, "Thanks."

Williams spoke up, "I've got good news, and bad news.   Bad news is, according to what Mike said those guys are probably headed to the same place we are.   The good news is, we don't have to walk there. You know those guys we just killed?   They were nice enough to leave us a truck."

"Why don't we just take the truck and drive to the border?" asked Mike.

"We can't just leave without trying to warn the Red Cross people about these guys."

"There's no way we can beat them there." said Mike.

"I know, but if I am their target and they think I am on foot they won't be expecting me until tomorrow sometime.   If I had to guess, I would say they'd try and set up an ambush for me."

"So you think, use the element of surprise?"   Mike started.

"Maybe but I haven't thought that far ahead just yet."

"So what do you suppose we do then Williams?" asked Mike.

"I say we go to the Red Cross camp and play it by ear.   We don't know how many of them there are or why they are after us but I would guess it has something to do with that truck we took out with the plane crash, considering they killed Lieutenant Gadsby when they found the weapons."

"Not us, you." Mike said. "They're after you."

"Whatever you decide, I'm with you." BB said.

Williams said, "I'm going to check and see what I can find outside." As he walked out the door he added, "We need to leave soon. They already have a head start and we don't know what their plans are when they get there."

BB looked at Mike and whispered, "I trust Williams. I just watched him take out three guys by himself. He thinks I got the last one but I never got a shot off. With the Lieutenant gone all we got is him. We don't have the training that he does and after today I trust him with my life."

"I understand." Mike said.

Williams walked back in and said, "We still have the RPG, five AK's, and three pistols. They were in the truck. I loaded the rest of our stuff and I'm ready to go when you are. I found a map in the truck. I can't read the writing but the doctor said something about railroad tracks and I think that this blue thing on the map indicates the Red Cross camp so I think we are somewhere in this area." He pointed on the map where he thought they were.

"We need to go and soon we're losing time fast."   The two men followed him out to the truck and they headed out toward what they thought was the right direction.

It was the third day since the disappearance of flight C-20973PYO and Major Haffick had not had any sleep and was on a caffeine diet that would kill most people.   He made his way up the stairs and through the busy office to the conference room for his update to the General.

He had no idea what he was going to tell the General.   They had found absolutely nothing in three days of searching. No plane, no crash site, no clues, no nothing.

Major Haffick entered the conference room.   As he took his seat General Omar said, "What have you found, Major?"

"Unfortunately, sir, satellite imagery still has nothing and I have people working around the clock.   We really need that Blackbird.

"It should be here this afternoon." said General Omar.

"Good."

The General continued, "I have increased our troop numbers on the border just in case and you need to prepare a briefing for the Blackbird pilot this afternoon.   I want him in the air by tomorrow."

"Yes sir."   Major Haffick said.

"Major."

"Yes General?"

"Get some sleep.   You look like run over shit."

"Will do sir, will do."

Captain Ishbad and his men arrived at the Red Cross camp at 11:20.   As he entered the small office of the clinic he said, "Hello Doctor."

The head Doctor asked, "What can we do for you sir?"

"We are just checking on the children and would like to offer any assistance that you may need."

"That is very kind of you sir.   The children are having their lunch right now. It is very rare that we have guests here at the orphanage. Is there anything we can do for you while you are visiting with us?"

"Is there anything we can provide such as, supplies for you?" the Captain asked sympathetically.

"We actually just received our monthly supply run yesterday."

The Captain stepped forward and leaned closer to the Doctor as if to tell him a secret.   "Actually Doctor I have a bit of a problem.   I am supposed to be reporting for a meeting but ran into a delay.   I need to notify my authorities, but I cannot get through."

He held up his cell phone to suggest bad reception and asked, "Would it be possible for us to use yours?"

The Doctor laughed.   "Why certainly." he said as he handed the Captain the satellite phone.   The Captain gave a puzzled look and asked, "Is this your only form of communication?"

The Doctor answered, "Well, being out here in such a remote location it's really the only thing that will work for us."

Captain Ishbad continued, "And you only have one of these?"

"For now...yes."

The Doctor's eyes widened as the Captain had obtained all the information that he needed and drew his side-arm.   He pointed it directly at the Doctors head and without expression or hesitation pulled the trigger.

The nurse screamed in terror and was quickly silenced with his second round.   He turned to his Lieutenant and said, "Sweep the area, no survivors.   Set up a perimeter and when the other American arrives kill him."

The Captain then took a Corporal with him and returned north to meet with the General and explain the situation.

Anna and Tamillee were sitting in her guest room.   Anna was admiring Tami's drawings when they heard the shots.   Two shots, the second preceded by a blood curdling scream which she recognized as Nurse Lynn, the head doctors lead assistant.

Anna rushed to the window where she discreetly looked through the small opening in the curtains.   As she peered out she noticed two armed Iranian military dressed men hurriedly walking across the courtyard where they began firing in the direction of the orphanage. The screams of children and several of the temps followed the rattle of the two AK-47's unleashing their fury on the un-expectant inhabitants.

Anna quickly turned and scanned the room for possible options. She looked up and realized the ceiling tiles.   She climbed to the top of her dresser and pushed one of the ceiling tiles up and to the side.

"Come quickly!" she urged Tamillee.   "Stay on the trusses she said as she hoisted the frightened girl into the diminutive crawlspace overhead.   She pulled herself up being careful not to step on the unsupported tiles.   "You have to be perfectly quiet no matter what happens, ok Tami." she said as she unlocked the room door to give the appearance that the room was uninhabited. She then hurriedly climbed into the ceiling with Tamillee and slid the displaced tile back into its rightful place.

The door burst open below and knowing the Arabic language, Anna understood the intruder as he shouted, "This one's empty too!" He left the room with the door still open and she whispered, "Just stay still and quiet until they leave."   Once again trying to refrain from crying Tamillee nodded.

Anna wondered why Iranian solders were attacking them.   She started to ask herself why she'd come this early in the year but realizing that by being early, she may very well have saved Tami's life broke her from the thought.   The thought of saving Tami gave her a small sense of relief.   She deliberated the thought that she might end up just like her parents, murdered in some remote refugee camp in a deficit, barren, country in the middle-east.   *"How about that for irony?"* she thought to herself.

The man was back, not in the room but standing outside the door. Someone was shouting something outside but it was too faint, she couldn't hear.   The man at the door suddenly shouted, "Put someone on the west ridge!   Stay out of site!   When the American gets here, let him get inside the camp!   He will most likely go to the clinic first!   Post one man in there!   If he comes out of the clinic; the sniper on the hill will take him out!"

"The American?"   Anna considered, maybe we are at war with Iran, but no.....he said American, singular, just one?   Why would they be targeting one single American?   Am I caught up in the middle of some

covert government operation, gone bad?   What would cause the Iranian military to slaughter an entire Red Cross camp in order to get one guy? She didn't know, but she knew it was not going to be getting quieter in the approaching moments.

The man was in the room now.   Anna could hear him moving around below them.   She looked at Tami who was terrified and held her index finger to her lips to remind Tami to stay perfectly quiet. Tami blinked her eyes and trapped tears simultaneously raced each other to her chin where they dropped onto her shirt which was already soaked from tears and sweat.   It was the hottest part of the day and being in the attic with no ventilation was even worse.

Another man entered the room and closed the door.   She recognized the sound of the curtain as he slid it open so that he could see out.   She guessed they had chosen her room as their position due to the fact that it was a clear shot from there to the clinic.   Already it seemed to be getting cooler and she was thankful for that. She listened as the men began to speak.

"Sir, if the American left the Doctors this morning he won't be here until the end of the day tomorrow."

"The Doctors?" she thought, was my Uncle involved?   All of a sudden she had a chill; she drew a lump in her throat, and felt slightly nauseated.   Had her Uncle.... *"Was he...Oh God, please no!"* she hoped. The other man answered, "That's why we have orders to stay here until

he arrives."

"What does the Captain want this American so bad for anyway?" griped one of the men.

"It's not the Captain, it's the General." said the Iranian Lieutenant.

"General Aveev?" asked the man curiously.

The Lieutenant was beginning to sound put out and said, "When the Captain hired you he didn't hire you to ask questions, he hired you to follow orders understand?"

The man replied, "Yes sir, I understand, I am sorry sir."

"Now, go make yourself useful and make sure there are no more kids running around this place."

"Yes sir!"

The door opened and closed again.   Then Anna heard the curtain slide again.   This time slower and not all the way.   She guessed he'd left it open just enough to observe the clinic.

As Anna listened for clues or sounds from her lofty refuge she debated on how Tamillee was handling this.   She thought about how she could make her feel better.   She thought of her facial expression and realized that the one she had on was showing as much terror as Tami's was.   In an attempt to comfort her, she resorted to the next best thing which was her angry face.   Not one she was very good at usually but she didn't seem to be having any trouble with it at this point in time.

She imagined herself heroically, crashing through the ceiling, overtaking the man and single-handedly taking out every one of the others and saving the day but who was she kidding?   She would hide in that ceiling for days, waiting for them to leave.   She was no hero, but she sure could use one right about now.

The trip from the doctors had been awkwardly quiet.   They'd been driving aimlessly through the dessert for almost an hour when they came across the railroad tracks.   Williams pulled the truck to the side of the road and reached into the glove compartment for the map.

"According to this map there should be a split in the tracks somewhere around here.   One set of tracks runs north and south, and the other runs to the southeast.   The doctor said that these tracks ran right by the Red Cross camp." he said pointing to the set of tracks running north and south on the map.

"If we can get those tracks we can just follow them south until we find the camp."

"What about that road?" asked Mike pointing at the map.

"They'll be watching the roads.   Our best bet is to stay off of the main roads."

Mike nodded, "I know that, what I meant was we haven't crossed it yet, and we would have had to have crossed it to get to that set of tracks."

"I suggest we keep driving west until we find tracks again and then head south."

"I agree." said Mike.

"You ok Mike?" asked BB.

"Yeah, Why?"

"That's the first time you agreed with anything he's said since the crash."

Mike looked at Williams, gave a little smile and said, "I guess I trust him too."

Williams returned the smile and spun a tire as he crossed the tracks and headed west.   "What's that?"   BB yelled as they bounced through the rocky terrain.   As luck would have it they had landed right at the railroad switching station.

They stopped again to look at the map.   "Ok, it looks like about twenty-five miles give or take a few, to the camp.   Now we need a plan."

"What do you have in mind?" asked BB.

"Well, If we just drive up they'll probably pick us off like target practice.   I say get close and leave the truck.   Go the rest of the way on foot and try to sneak up on them undetected."

"Won't they be watching the tracks?"   Mike asked ambiguously.

"I'm hoping that they will have more focus on the east side of the camp since that's where they expect me to come from."

"Ahh, the element of surprise again right?   They're expecting you from the east; you come in from the west.   I get it."   Mike said comprehensively.

"Well, times a tickin'."   BB said.

"You're right BB.   Let's go." said Williams as he put the truck in gear and this time spinning both wheels.   They drove south following the tracks for what Williams judged to be about twenty miles and stopped once again.

"This is probably close enough.   We should walk from here." Williams said as he shut the motor off and stepped out of the truck. He continued with, "Ok, Mike, are you going to be up to this?"

"Well I'm not staying here alone." answered Mike as he looked over at BB and asked, "How about you, BB?"
"I'm as ready as I'm gonna get." He answered.   Williams reached back inside the truck and grabbed his bag and one of the rifles.   He then walked around the front of the truck to the tracks and as he kicked the rail knocking some clotted dirt from his boot he said, "Well, let's do this."

CHAPTER 6

"AN UNLIKELY HERO"

The first thing Williams saw as he approached the camp was the four thousand gallon water tank because it was the tallest thing on the compound.   The second thing he saw was the Iranian sniper lying in the prone facing in at the camp and as he had hoped completely ignoring anything to his rear.

The terrain was much the same as it was around the doctors' house which made it surprisingly easy to move undetected around to a good position directly behind the unsuspecting sniper.

"Stay here.   I have to take him out first and I have to do it quietly.   BB, you cover for me.   It looks like he is alone but if someone sees me you have to take him out with that AK because I'll be busy with that one.   You got me?"

"I got you." BB answered.

Williams looked at Mike and tried to think of some way he could help.   Finally he just said, "Mike you help him watch, ok?"

"Ok." replied Mike shivering with nervousness.

Williams turned and began to make his way toward the

complacent sniper, knife in hand.   He found it astonishingly easy to walk quietly in the fine sand as he closed on the snipers position.

He was right on top of him now but he noticed that the sniper had his finger on the trigger.   Even if he could keep him from shouting *what if the guy squeezed off a round?*   It would alarm everyone in the camp.

As luck would have it the sniper suddenly took his trigger hand and reached around to scratch an itch.   Now was the opportunity that Williams needed and he may not get another.

He leaped onto the sniper and simultaneously shoved his face into the dirt, thus preventing him from shouting an alarm, and plunged the knife directly into his head just above where the neck ends and the head begins centered, almost between the ears.

During his briefings at the beginning of his deployment he'd been taught that if you wanted to kill someone and have no reflexive responsiveness afterward, all you had to do was aim for the teeth. Almost directly at the back of the throat is what is called the Abdulla oblongata.   It controls all the brain waves that the brain sends to the rest of the body, and if it is severed the body is rendered 100% motionless instantly.

Williams plan was just that.   Sever the oblongata, quickly and effectively.   It worked.   The man was completely still, immediately. He almost couldn't believe that it worked.   He looked back at BB and Mike and motioned them forward.   Mike started to gag when he saw the blood which was still being pumped from the hole in the man's head but choked it back and just tried to avoid looking.

"I thought you weren't trained for this?"   BB asked noticing the effective kill.

"I'm not but what little the Army did give in basic skills I at least paid attention to."   Williams replied.

"Well I'm certainly glad you did." added Mike who was turning pale very quickly.

"Are you all right Mike?"   Williams asked.

"No, not really.   I didn't expect to see any action in my line of work when I volunteered for this job.   I'll make it though I just need to let it all sink in that's all."

"This is not the time to be getting faint on me all right Mike.   If you don't think you can handle it, you need to stay up here ok."

"No," Mike said as he took a deep breath I can handle this."

"Are you sure?   You don't exactly look too convincing."

"I'm fine, I promise.   I'm right behind you.   Just tell me what to do."

Williams looked at BB and raised his brow slightly.

"I'm ready.   Let's do it."   BB said.

Williams positioned himself closer to the ridge to peer down into the camp.   He turned and looked behind him at the horizon.   It was almost two in the afternoon and it was going to be very difficult to move

LOST IN THE STORM

down the steep incline without being noticed.   Williams thought if they could just wait about an hour the sun would be directly behind them and would make it more difficult to see someone moving down the hill side.

He squinted against the relentless sunlight to see into the camp. It looked as if it were abandoned.   He scanned the entire premises. There was no movement, no children running around outside playing, nothing.   It looked like a ghost town.   He had a bad feeling. Something wasn't right.

The SR-71 Blackbird roared down the runway and was directed to the tarmac where the pilot exited the plane and was escorted into the building.

Major Haffick checked the clock on the wall as he sat in his office. There was a knock at the door.

"It's open!" shouted Major Haffick from his chair behind his cluttered desk.   The door opened and a dark headed girl with glasses stepped in.

"Sir, he's here...The pilot from Aviano Air Base." said the young

Airman First Class.

"The long range surveillance guy?" asked Major Haffick.

"Yes sir, he's in the terminal waiting area."

"Have him escorted to the conference room please."

"Yes sir." she said as she pulled the door to.

The Major would have had the pilot sent to his office for his briefing but his office was a wreck and frankly, he didn't even like being in his office.   Besides, the conference room was just down the hall and a much more professional environment.   Not to mention, it was a lot cleaner.

As he entered the room the young captain was standing in the corner analyzing the large wall map of Iran.   Beside him was a small carry bag.   Major Haffick pushed the door to.   As he switched the light on he asked, "Is that all your gear?"

Startled by the light, the Captain turned and said, "I prefer to travel light sir.   The rest of my gear is in the plane."

"Captain Dayton, is it?" asked the Major.

"At your service sir." said the young pilot.

"Have a seat Captain." said Major Haffick as he gestured toward one the chairs.

As Captain Dayton sat Major Haffick began, "We have had a plane go down.   We believe they are somewhere in the north region of Iran. What we need for you to do is make several sweeps of the country and gather as much info as you can."

"What am I looking for, sir?"

"It was a C-130 cargo. She was light, with 13 personnel hitching a ride and two pilots.   They were flying dry and we expect there wouldn't be much to burn so don't count on smoke.   It's also been three days so if there had been a fire it would probably be gone by now. You'll most likely be looking for strewn wreckage"

"I understand.   When do you need me wheels up?" he asked.

"Zero six hundred hours tomorrow morning.   Airman First Class Bales is outside.   She'll show to your quarters."

"Thank you Sir." He picked up his bag and retreated to the hallway where he was met by the Airman First Class and they disappeared down the hall.

The sun was behind them now.   Williams looked over at BB and asked, "Are you ready?"

"What's the plan, Sarge?" he asked back.

"I haven't seen any movement so we need to move carefully. Once the first shot is fired, everyone will know we're here, so be ready, and whatever you do, if there are civilians try not to fire at them by mistake."

"Do we split up, or stay together?" asked Mike.

"I don't know?   That depends on what we find once we get down there.   To begin with we'll stay together but remember, if we're grouped together we are a larger, more obvious target."

He looked back at the camp and studied the layout.   The railroad crossed between them and the camp.   The first thing they would come to was the generators fuel tank.

Then there was what appeared to be a small storage building, the generator, water tower, and waste water tank.   In the center of the camp was the latrine, judging by the water and return water lines running to and from it.

At the south end of the camp was a fairly large building that resembled a small motel.   Straight ahead from their position but to the north end of the camp was a large building that he guessed was the orphanage.

Directly across from the orphanage was a small building labeled with the Red Cross sign.   He thought to him-self, *"That must be the clinic."*   To its right was the tiny greenhouse.   There was a large truck parked just beyond the greenhouse and a commercial van backed up to the second door of the building at the south end of the camp.

There were no windows on the backside of the orphanage building which made it impossible to see in but more importantly it served as a very good cover position for them.   Looking between the

119

water tower and the waste water tank Williams could see that all the curtains appeared to be pulled closed on the south building.

Suddenly the clinic door opened and a single Iranian soldier came out. He made his way across the court yard to the south building and went into the second room. Williams continued to watch the door. The man emerged after a few minutes and returned to the clinic where he disappeared through the door of the tiny building.

Williams knew there was at least one guy in the clinic and there was a good chance there was someone in that second room of the south building, but that couldn't be all there was. He looked down at his shoulder and remembered the hole in it. Suddenly the pain seemed to get worse and then better. Not gone, but numb, like something was replacing the pain momentarily. He thought to himself, it must be the adrenalin.

"Ok," he said, "Here's the plan. "Mike, how good can you shoot?"

"I don't know? I've never shot anything before, unless you count video games."

"Do you at least know how to aim and reload?" Williams asked enthusiastically.

"Yes, I was with BB and the Lieutenant last night when Lieutenant Gadsby was showing BB how to shoot." answered Mike.

"Do you think you can hit anything from here?"

"I can try."

"Ok, Mike you stay here and watch our backs.   It'll be easier for you to shoot from here one-handed.   If you see anyone that we don't, and you can tell they are enemy, at least distract them with cover fire."

"Ok."

"How much ammo do you have?"

Mike held up a magazine and said, "I have six of these."

"Good."   Williams said. "That should last awhile."

"How much do you have, BB?"

BB said, "I only have three."

"That should be more than enough.   Just try not to waste any. That goes for both of you."

They nodded.   "BB, you follow me down the hill.   When we get to the bottom, cross the tracks and you go to the right end of that big building to the north."   Williams said pointing."

BB continued nodding.

Williams turned his attention to Mike and said, "Keep your eye on that building to the right where that guy went in a while ago.   If anyone comes out, Mike, you start shooting."

Mike also nodded again.

"BB, if Mike doesn't hit anything you take them out, but stay behind something solid for cover."

"Ok, I got ya."

"Nobody shoots until I do, unless they spot you."   Looking at Mike he added, "It's important that you stay calm and think straight.   If you freak out, you could just make things worse for all of us." Williams checked his own AK-47 and double checked his 9mm then looked at BB.

"Let's go." he said.

As they stood and BB started to step forward Williams looked back and added, "Mike, you can do this.   I trust you."   He stepped forward and he and BB worked their way to the bottom of the hill.

They stopped at the fuel tank where Williams checked that the coast was still clear, and then motioned for BB to follow.   As they came to the small shed he noticed it was pad locked and assured BB that it was safe to pass.

At the back of the building he thought was the orphanage Williams pointed to the south corner for BB to take the position and he took his position at the opposite corner where he could see the clinic. The door to the clinic was standing open and Williams could see that there were two soldiers inside both wielding AK-47's.   He rolled to the right putting his back to the wall.

He then half stood and quickly, but quietly made his way to BB. As he began to tell BB what he had seen a door opened on the Southside of the orphanage just around the corner from where they were.   They froze and could here footsteps as the soldier walked across the gravel to the latrine.

Williams whispered, "Stay here.   If you hear gunshots watch for that guy and take him down before he gets back to this building if you don't hear gunshots let him go.   I'm going to try and take as many as I can quietly."

"Ok, only shoot if I hear you shootin'."   BB repeated.

"That's right."   Williams said standing and peeking around the corner of the building.   He didn't see anyone so he stepped around the corner and cautiously walked to the door.

The door had a small dirty window in it and as he peered in he could see a second soldier inside.   The man's attention was focused out the window toward the clinic so Williams tried to open the door quietly. The door squeaked as he opened it and he prepared to fire.   Surprisingly the man didn't seem to have heard the door or perhaps he just thought it was his partner returning.

Williams glanced around the room.   It was an open bay and it appeared as if there were no partitioned off areas in the entire building. The man seemed to be alone.   Williams was in the open and knew if the man turned around his stealth would be terminated.   He knew the other guy would probably be returning soon so he had to move quickly he took the knife and approached the soldier looking out the window.

Just like before he thought.

Both hands.....

One motion.....

Left hand over the mouth... knife in the right.

This time he plunged the knife into the man's throat and immediately twisted it.

Instead of pulling the man's body backward he leaned him forward where he gargled and spat as he struggled for his last bit of life. *Hurry,* Williams thought, *Hurry up and die before the other guy returns.* The man's body finally went limp.

Williams staying low so not to be noticed through the window that the man was watching out of, propped the man's body forward to make it appear as though he'd fallen asleep.   He hurriedly made his way back to the door and waited for the other guy's arrival.

As he waited he scanned the room and was shocked at what he beheld.   He hadn't noticed before because he was too busy watching the man at the window.   The room was lined with beds.   At the far end was an open kitchen.   There was a long table between the kitchen and the beds.

It looked as if they were just slaughtered as they ate Williams thought as he observed the lifeless bodies of the children, some still sitting upright at the table.   He began to feel enraged but the sound of footsteps outside brought him back to his senses.   The man was returning.   He readied his knife still wet with blood from the first guy.

As the man entered and saw his partner who appeared to be sleeping on the job, he began to say something when Williams lunged at his back.   He overshot his mark with the knife and desperate to keep the man silent, locked his arm around the man's neck and held on as tightly as he could.   He thought to himself, *Thank God he's small.*

The man struggled for what seemed like forever before finally starving for oxygen he passed out and suddenly became heavy. Realizing the man was unconscious Williams loosened his grip and as he released the man's body ran the knife across his neck cutting it across the Adams apple and looking at the blood puddling on the floor he assumed he had found an artery.

As he looked again at the carnage he felt cold and angry that anyone could perform such a ruthless act on innocent children.   He momentarily felt the urge to hunt down the remaining perpetrators and make them pay for this terrible thing they'd done.

He looked at his hand which was covered in blood.   He wondered for a second if it was his or theirs when he remembered his shoulder.   All of a sudden the pain returned to his shoulder and he felt as if he would scream in pain.

He looked through the window of the door and once he was comfortable that no one could see he cracked the door and whispered to

BB, "Hey, it's me.   Don't shoot."

"What's up?" asked BB as Williams shuffled around the corner and knelt against the wall.

"There were two of them in there and........"

"What Sarge?" BB asked while continuing to watch around the corner of the building.

"They killed all those kids BB.   All of them.   Just... just... slaughtered."

"Bastards." BB said with a look of disgust.

"I think I can get those two in the clinic from the other end of this building but I don't know how many there might be in that third building."

"How about you just take them two.   I'll watch the other building and if anybody comes out I'll blow their ass away."

"You'll have to move over there so you can see."   Williams said pointing at the back of the latrine.

"Ok."   BB answered.

"You don't think Mike would hit you by mistake if you go over there do you?"

"I'm a two-hundred and seventy pound black man.   How could he mistake me for one of them?"

"I don't mean like that.   I mean do you think his aim could be that bad?"

"Oh, nah, he's got to be better than that."

"If you trust him I guess I will too.   Just keep your eyes open. You go ahead and go.   Give me a thumb's up when you're ready and I'll go down there and start a fight."

"Just don't get killed, ok Sarge."   BB said as he stood to his feet. Keeping low BB ran to the backside of the small latrine building and peered around the corner at the second room of the south building. Once he was happy that he could see everything clear he turned and gave Williams a thumb's up.

Williams returned the gesture and made his way down the rear of the orphanage to the corner where he'd seen the two soldiers in the clinic earlier.

This time he could only see one but all the same he propped his rifle on the air-conditioning unit at the end of the building and took aim at the first soldier.   He mumbled aloud, *I hope this thing shoots straight.*

He slowed his breathing and closed his left eye.   He steadied the rifle, set his front sights on the target, and aligned his rear sights with the front sights.   He aimed for the chest and slowly squeezed the trigger.

The blast startled him and he noted a direct hit.   He watched the door where the stunned but observant second soldier appeared at the door and it seemed as though he had no clue where the shot came from.

A second shot startled Williams and then several shots one after another.   It must be BB he thought but either way it caused the second soldier in the clinic to step out just enough. Williams closed his left eye again, took aim, again a direct hit. He watched the door for a moment and there was no movement. BB continued to fire, two, then three, then two more shots.

Williams ran back to the corner of the building and then darted to where he'd left BB. "What's going on BB?"

"There's one in there!" yelled BB as he fired another three shots at the window of the second room of the south building. Two of which landed below the window splintering the wooden frame.

"Is that the only one you've seen?"

"Yeah, he tried to bring his ass out but I started blastin' at him and he ducked back inside."

"Ok, give me about thirty seconds and then stop firing and stay behind something."

BB discharged two more rounds and asked, "What you got in mind sarge?"

"I'm going to kill that son of a bitch." Williams replied as if he was surprised that BB even had to ask.

Williams crawled around and positioned himself cattycornered from BB's position and BB stopped firing. After about ten seconds of silence, and just as Williams had expected the guy in the room looked out, raised his rifle and began firing at BB's corner. Williams took aim and fired one single shot in the chest.

Williams rolled over to see BB right behind him.   "Are you ok?" BB asked. "Yeah. You?"   BB grinned.   "Not a scratch.   What now?" he asked.

"Stay right behind me.   We have to do the scary part now."

As Williams started to walk around the side of the building BB with a puzzled look on his face said, "And that wasn't scary?"   He then realized Williams was walking away and scurried to catch him.

As they approached the south building BB asked, "So what's the scary part?" not really wanting the answer.

Williams speaking over his shoulder said, "We have to check all these rooms and make sure we got all of them."

"I got your back."   BB said peeking around Williams as if to hide behind him.

When they came to the first door Williams said, "You open the door from the side.   I'll kick it open and check that it is clear.   If I jump to the side it's because I ran out of ammo or it didn't fire when I pulled the trigger.   In that case you assume there is something in the room and you just step in and start firing, corner to corner ok."

"Ok." BB said nervously.

BB turned the knob on the first door and before he got it open Williams startled him by kicking the door open and stepping forward sweeping the room for any targets.   After he was sure it was clear he stepped back and calmly said, "It's clear."

The third room they checked had the bathroom door closed and Williams said, "Ok, this one's a little different.   We have to do the same thing but we have to do it inside."

"Gotcha." replied BB finally getting the hang of things.

The bathroom was clear.   Williams realized that the bathroom led to an adjoining room and said, "One more time BB."   After clearing the adjoining room he said, "We need to go back and check the last two the same way.   They checked the first two over and moved on to the fourth.

"Be ready BB, this is the one that guy is in."   Williams kicked open the door and noticed that the room was riddled with holes and the man was laid back on the bed with blood splattered across the newly made bed spread.

As they made their way to the bathroom the man moved.   He'd drawn a pistol when BB fired three shots into the man's chest.   They stood poised for a moment and Williams asked, "Are you good?" BB just nodded because he couldn't speak.   After checking the bathroom and the next room, they started out when Williams grabbed BB's collar. "What?"   BB asked as Williams traded places with him and put his back to the wall right at the doorway.

"Mike, it's just us coming out, don't shoot ok!"

"Ok!" was heard from up on the hill and they exited the room to finish clearing the building.   After clearing the final room Williams said,

"We need to check the clinic and then we'll be ok."

BB still unable to speak nodded and they made their way to the clinic.   They cleared the clinic the same way and once the four small rooms were cleared they took note of the Doctor's and Nurse's bodies and returned to the center of the camp where Williams shouted, "It's all clear Mike!   Come on down!"   Mike made his way to the bottom of the hill and asked, "Well, now what?"

"First, Mike, you go to the clinic and see if you can find a way to contact someone and let them know we're here.   Me and BB will go see if we can figure out why these guys wanted us dead so bad."

"How are you going to do that?" asked Mike.

"I don't know, but the guy that was held up in that room looked to be the one in charge so we'll check things out in there and you see what you can do, ok."

"Ok just stay where you can hear me alright."   Mike replied.

"We'll be right in that room and we can see you from there. Don't worry everything is clear now."

Williams and BB walked back to the room and Williams was checking the man's pockets when BB said, "What was that?" while looking at the ceiling.   Williams asked, "What was what?"   He looked at BB.   He was backing toward the door and pointing at the ceiling and said, "The ceiling is moving."

Williams, confused looked up at where BB was pointing and they heard a faint voice from above say, "Don't shoot, please!" Despite the request Williams drew his 9mm and backed away as the ceiling tile was kicked loose from above.   Again and louder this time they heard, "Please, don't shoot.   I'm American."   Williams and BB looked at each other and BB mouthed the word, *"American".*

A small foot appeared from the hole in the ceiling followed by what they both noticed was a considerably nice shaped body and topped with a beautiful face.   She knelt atop the dresser and asked, "Are you here to help?"   BB answered, "Well, we ain't gonna hurt you, if that's what you're asking."

She then turned back to the hole in the ceiling and said, "It's ok Tami, we're safe now."   The two men looked at each other again and both wondered what they had gotten themselves into.   "I'm Anna and this is Tamillee.   Who are you and where is everyone else?" she asked almost crying.

"Ma'am........You and her are it.   Everyone else is....."

Before he could finish Anna's knees became weak and she had to hold onto the dresser to keep from falling to the floor. "The....the children?" she cried.

"I'm sorry miss, but they..." Williams noticed the terrified look on the little girls face and said, "Let's find a better place to talk." as he walked to the door where BB was already standing.

As they entered the next room Anna continued, barely controlling her sobs, "I come here every......" Williams interrupted, "We know Ma'am."

"Just call me Anna, and what do mean, you know?"

"Anna," Williams continued, "You may want to sit down for this."

Anna's heart sank she knew what was coming.   They were going to tell her that her uncle was dead too.   She felt as if she would burst into uncontrollable tears.   Then she caught a glimpse of Tami out of the corner of her eye and knew she had to be strong for her if nothing else. She fought to control her emotion as best she could.

Williams started, "I'm Sergeant Williams.   This is BB and Mike is in the clinic looking for a way to call for help."

Anna interrupted, "The SAT Phone."

"The what?" asked BB.

Anna explained, "The satellite phone is the only means of communication they have here."

"No internet, no radio, just a SAT Phone?" asked Williams.

"That's it."   Anna answered.

Williams continued, "Anyway, we were supposed to be flying home from Iraq and somehow our plane went down about one hundred miles northeast of here.   We hiked from the crash to your Uncle's house.   He helped us out and BB and I here were on our way here on foot when......"

"When what?"   Anna asked, her voice cracking with the fear that she already knew what was coming next.

"When we heard the gunshots we ran as fast as we could but we were too late."

She began to lose control again and as she wept BB added, "We got those Bastards though."

Williams kicked BB and nodded toward Tamillee. "Oh. Sorry." BB whispered.

Williams continued, "Your uncle had told us about you and the Red Cross camp so we came here after we left your Uncle's."

"Why did those people attack us and why were they after you." Anna asked.

"According to Mike who was hiding at your Uncle's and overheard them talking to the Lieutenant who was also killed at your Uncle's, they were here to try and ambush me.   They thought I was alone and apparently, their wanting to kill me has something to do with some weapons that we stumbled across at our crash site."

"Who is General Aveev and this Captain?" she asked.

"We don't know anything.......wait... what do know that we don't?" Williams asked.

"I overheard the guy in the other room talking with one of his subordinates and they made mention of a General Aveev and some Captain.   It sounded like the Captain worked for the General and they didn't say anything about any weapons."

"Well, those weapons are what we think got the Lieutenant and your.....we think that's what got them killed.   Because, according to Mike right after they found the weapons we'd taken from the crash they shot them on the spot and came here for me."

"Why didn't you just leave the weapons where you found them?" she asked.

"First of all Miss, we didn't know if we were in hostile territory or not, and secondly, they aren't after us for taking the weapons they're after us for seeing them."

"So you think they are illegal or something?"

"Something like that."   Williams answered.

Mike walked in and with a dumbfounded expression asked, "Did I miss something?"

"Mike, this is Anna.   Anna, Mike." said Williams.

Anna slowly regaining her composure continued, "So, what is your plan now?"

Williams looked at Mike and asked, "What did you find Mike?"

"Mike held up a mangled resemblance of a phone and said this is all I found."

"Can you fix it?" asked Anna.

"I take it that means there's only one?"   Mike asked back.

"Yes." she said reluctantly while wiping tears away with her shirtsleeve.

"Then we're screwed." Mike said bluntly.

Williams broke in and said, "In that case the plan is the same as it was when we started out. We head for the Iraqi border where we know there are American forces."

"That's it, that's your plan. Run for the border?" Anna raved.

"Unless you have a better one!" Williams insisted.

Anna was speechless. She realized that she couldn't think of a better plan and she *knew* where she was. They didn't have a clue where they were and at least they came up with that much. She looked at her hands, which is what she always did when she was embarrassed or stumped, then she looked at Williams and asked, "So is Rambo here in charge?"

"You know, that's the second time in three days I've been called Rambo! If anyone else has any better ideas, by all means share them now!" No one spoke, and after a short moment of awkward silence Anna asked, "What do you suggest now?" Everyone looked at Williams and it was clear that they had all if only silently, agreed that he was the decision maker from here on out.

"You said the guy said something about a Captain and a General. That means these guys were just a bunch of pawns following orders. If there is someone bigger than these guys behind this he's not going to be happy when he comes to check on his men and finds that we have taken them out. He will probably come after us with a whole lot more than just six guys next time."

"Then I suggest we get a move on before they get here." groaned Mike.

"Yes, that's exactly what I suggest and we have a new navigator." Williams said pointing at Anna.

"Why me?" she asked.

"Because, you're more familiar with the area than we are."

"Yeah but once we get to the mountains you're on your own again. I've never been any further west than the base of the mountains and I don't know any of those roads or trails."

"We'll cross that bridge when we get there." Williams said as he turned for the door. "We need to gather all the supplies we can and we will take this van. It looks dependable enough."

"It is." Anna interrupted. "It's the van I always take to my Uncle's and we've never had any trouble out of it."

"Good, now let's see what kind of supplies we can round up. Anna, can I call you Anna?"

"Yes." she replied.

"Where do they keep supplies here that we could use?"

"In the shed, behind the orphanage. I'll get the key."

"Thanks," he said as she brushed past him with Tamillee holding her hand and following.

"Yeah, sure." she snarled back under her breath.

Once she'd left BB asked, "What are we gonna do with a woman and a little girl?"

"We're going to take them with us.   What do you mean?" Williams asked.

BB frowned and added "I mean, won't they slow us down?"

"Not any more than the Lieutenant would have, besides what would you tell her?   Oh, well, you're going to have to stay here and wait on the bad guys.   Really, come on BB."

"I guess your right on that one." answered BB.

Williams met Anna at the shed and she tossed him the keys as she walked up.   Out of habit and reflex he caught the keys with his right hand and tried to hide a grimace.   As he tried to put the key in the lock she noticed the blood on his hand and that he was shaking, from the pain she guessed.

Despite her feelings toward the hardcore, egoistic, killer type, which she'd judged him to be, she had a soft spot for the suffering in general.   As she reached at his hand she said, "You're bleeding." Williams out of pride or possibly just stubbornness pulled his arm away and said, "It's nothing."

"If you're hurt I can take a look." she continued.

"No really, it's fine."   Williams repeated not wanting her to know the truth.

She stepped closer and insisted, "Just let....."

Williams snatched his arm away again, this time the pain showing obviously, and said through gritted teeth, "It's not mine."

Anna's face grew pale with the sudden realization that the blood on his arm belonged to one of the men he'd just killed and the concerned look on her face turned to a solemn frown.

As she stood frozen in her stance, Williams opened the door and entered the shed where he grabbed a handful of items and walked away without a word, leaving her there in shock.

Captain Ishbad was beginning to get concerned.   His Lieutenant at the Doctors had not checked in since that morning.   He walked across the parking lot and into the large warehouse.   The general was waiting inside.

"How's the search going?" asked the General as Captain Ishbad sat at the small table.

"Which one?" asked Captain Ishbad.

"The plane first."

"So far they have searched all day and there has been no sign of any crash and as far as the American goes I have six personnel at the Red Cross camp waiting to intercept.   After he's taken care of I'll make it look like a rebel attack and the same with the Doctors.

One of the extra trucks from the desert search had arrived to report a piece of debris that they believed could've been a part of off an American aircraft. After getting the coordinates for the location of the find the General said, "You take the two trucks with you Captain, and check on your team at the Doctors. I'll have another team meet me in the desert to look for the plane."

"Right away sir." said Captain Ishbad as he stood to exit the warehouse. Just as he was ordered he gathered two trucks and returned south where he would go to the doctors and send the other truck to assist with the clean-up at the Red Cross camp.

CHAPTER 7

"THE CHASE"

Williams turned the key and the van started without hesitation. "Mike, BB, you two get in the back I need her to show me where to go."   Mike gave BB a yeah right look and they loaded into the middle seat of the van.

Williams reached across and opened the passenger door to find himself eye to eye with Tamillee.   He sat back up and Anna nodded for Tami to get in.   Williams checked the rearview mirror where and noticed Mike feigning hysterical laughter.   Mike looked at BB and whispered, "At least he still gets to sit next to a chick."

BB answered, "I'm pretty sure she can hear you."

Anna cut her eyes at Mike as she struggled with her medical bag, which she finally managed to squeeze between her legs and the seat. As she slammed the door Williams looked up to see another Iranian truck pulling into the drive.

"Get down!"   Williams shouted.   As the truck pulled to a stop at the door of the clinic, he peered over the dash to see what was happening. He knew it would only be a matter of seconds before they would be rampantly searching the camp. He had to think of something, and fast.

The man came out of the clinic yelling and waving his hands, pointing and directing. The three remaining men spread out to start the search. Two of the men started directly toward their position and one for the orphanage.

As they approached Williams said, "Ok, everyone hang on and stay down." He closed his eyes, gathered his thoughts, and sat straight up. The two men approaching froze for a moment and before they had time to realize what was happening, Williams floored it.

He aimed the van directly at the two approaching men and they had no choice but to dive out of the way. He then headed for the clinic and pointed the van at the rear fender of the Iranian's truck just enough for a clip. He yelled, "Hang on!"

As the man riddled the van shattering the right side windows the van smashed the rear of the truck sending it lurching forward at the gunman standing at the clinic entrance. The man retreated into the clinic to avoid being crushed by his own truck.

Williams sat up pulling the truck back onto the road and speeding away. Anna shook the glass out of her hair and leaned over to ask Tami if she was alright.

"Are you guys ok back there?" Williams asked checking his

mirrors and pushing the side view mirror on his side out just a little.

"Yeah," answered BB as he brushed the glass off his shoulder. Mike spouted, "Wonderful, I'm just wonderful."

Anna now comfortable that Tami was ok looked up at Williams and screamed, "You could've gotten us killed back there with your little hero stunt, you know that!"

Williams replied, "Would you rather I had tried to reason with them?"

"At least we're all alive." BB said. "We need to worry about where we're going next right now because they're gonna be comin' after us in a minute and that truck is probably faster than this van."

Anna looked at BB and then back at Williams.

"About a mile ahead." she said, "There's a dirt trail. It leads west to the mountains. It's open but like I said, it's dirt so it's going to leave a dust trail for them to follow."

"As long as we can stay ahead of them I'll think of something later. At least we got a little head start." Williams said checking his mirror again.

The Iranians scurried to their feet and ran to the truck. One of the men shouted, "They took out the antenna!"

"Check the other truck!" yelled the Lieutenant, as he slammed the handset against the dash.

"This is the one that's busted!" exclaimed the radio guy.

"Ok, you, and you come with me."   The Lieutenant said, pointing to the radio man and one of the other Corporals.

"You stay here and tell the Captain what happened when he arrives." he said to the remaining Corporal.

"Sir, yes sir!" replied the soldier, as he stepped aside for the Lieutenant to get into the other truck.

"Go!"   He shouted and turned to the radio guy.   "Can you fix this thing?" he asked pointing at the radio in the dash.

"I'll see what I can do!" he answered back as the truck sped out of the driveway.

"Do you see anything, Mike?" asked Williams.

"Just dust, lots of dust." answered Mike.

"Let me know if you see anything ok."

"Don't worry, I will." Assured Mike as he squinted his eyes at a poor attempt to see through the rear glass of the van.

"Ok, your, our turn is right up here." interrupted Anna.

"Where?" asked Williams.

"Right there, Right there!" she shouted as he almost past it.

As Williams fishtailed off the dusty road onto the almost unnoticeable trail Mike exclaimed, "You have got to be kidding! This is like trying to ride a bicycle on the beach!"

"The van will make it. Just don't go too slow." Anna replied.

"I don't think going too slow will be a problem." said BB sarcastically.

"Can you see anything now, Mike?" repeated Williams.

Looking back the direction from which they'd just come, Mike squinted again to see. "Yeah there's another cloud of dust about......oh... a mile." BB leaned over to see and shouted, "Their about three miles back sarge!"

Mike looked at BB and said, "I don't know. I don't drive for a living."

"Thanks BB. If we can keep a good distance, we can either loose them in the mountains or at least set an ambush for them." Williams said looking back to see for himself.

"There you go again, wanting to set up an ambush. Is killing people all you know how to do?" Anna protested.

Williams gave her an unsettled look and couldn't think of a good answer so he just looked back forward and hoped she would just drop the issue. He thought to himself, *"That's just my luck. I save the girls life and she's a bleeding heart who hates anything in a uniform."*

She thought to herself, *"He did save my life. Am I being too hard*

145

on him or should I hate the guy?" To be on the safe side she decided to just not like him for now and she stared out the window with her arms crossed to show her otherwise obvious discontent.

Tamillee who had not said a word since their discovery at the camp suddenly asked, "Why do those people want to kill us?"

Surprised at her decision to speak, as was the whole group, Anna looked at Tami and said, "Honey, they're not after us. We didn't do anything wrong." Cutting her eyes at Williams she added, "They're after these guys...." Williams returned a look of disbelief as she finished, ".....but we aren't going to let anyone hurt you ok."

"Ok." she said as she placed her head on Anna's shoulder.

Mike said, "I hate to be negative all the time but it looks like they're getting closer. Can this thing go any faster?"

"I'm going as fast as I can." Williams answered while looking down at the speedometer.

"I can't read this stupid speedometer because it's in kilometers." he complained as he attempted to wipe the dust off the instrument panel. Instead he just smeared it.

Anna leaned over to see. "We're going about sixty-five or seventy." she said as she sat back up straight.

While he was still looking at the dash he noticed the temp light was on. "Does this temp light come on often?"

Anna looked at him confoundedly and said, "No."

"A stray bullet must have hit the radiator and is causing the engine to run hot.   We might not make it all the way like this."

"Oh now you're a professional mechanic and a hero.   I guess today's just our lucky day."   Anna said.

Williams chose not to argue and just kept driving.   As he drove he began to notice white steam coming from under the hood.   He looked at Anna and then Tami and said, "She may need to move."

"Why?" asked Anna.

"If this thing locks up on us something is going to give.   It could just be the driveshaft but I have seen transmissions completely come out from under vehicles.   The only other thing that could happen is the clutch might go out.   If that happens, it's got to go somewhere and that somewhere is usually up."

"Where is this clutch?" asked Mike.

"Pointing at the floor directly beneath Tami's feet he said, "Right under there."

Tami, understanding most of what he said climbed into Anna's lap and they shared the seat belt.   Williams turned to BB and Mike and said, "You two may want to buckle up too, just in case nothing gives, and we go from seventy to zero in a matter of seconds."

Just as he finished his warning they heard a hissing sound followed by a pop.   They gazed at one another and abruptly it sounded like fireworks were going off right under their feet. Williams checked the shifter. *Nothing.*

"As the truck came to a stop Williams shouted, "Everybody get into those hills."

"What are you going to do?" asked Anna trying to hide a concerned tone in her voice.

"I don't exactly know but if anything happens to me you don't stop until you make the border.   If these guys still think I am alone they may not follow you."

As they rushed to the cover of the rocky terrain Williams quickly scanned the area.   They had broken down in an ideal spot for a counter ambush he thought as he took note of the narrow pass they had just come down.   There were hints of plant life with small shrubs and even a tree here and there but scarcely placed.   Parallel to the van in the middle of the road was a large rocky formation.   He knew what he wanted to do and immediately grabbed the RPG tube and realized that BB had taken all the rounds.

"BB!" he yelled.

BB's head appeared from behind a nearby ridge. "Yeah?"

Williams held up the RPG tube and said, "The rounds!"

"Here catch!"   BB said as he tossed a round toward Williams.

"No don't........." Williams had heard that RPG rounds would still go off occasionally even if thrown.   He ran and dove to catch the round before it hit the ground.

"You good?" BB asked.

Williams sighed and motioned for BB to stay down. He ran to his chosen position across from the van and as he waited, loaded the round into the end of the tube. He thought to himself, *One shot, better make it count.* He wished for a moment he'd gotten a second round but in his rush he had not considered the possibility that he may miss with the first one.

He heard the truck as it came to a stop about 100 meters away. *Closer*, he thought. *I need them closer.* He glanced around the rock to see what they were doing. He could tell that there were three bodies in the truck and he thought about firing quick in the event they might dismount the vehicle and the RPG would be a waste and he'd have to shoot it out anyway.

The truck began moving again and he knew that the grenade was timed with a fuse and had to go a certain distance before it became active. He stepped out, but just enough to see and not too quickly in hopes that their attention would be focused on the van. He took aim, *the grill or the window? It shouldn't matter. Just don't miss.* He pulled the trigger.

The grenade cut through the air leaving a stream of smoke in its shortly inhabited trail and planted itself right above the bumper. "Yeah!" he exclaimed, surprised himself that his target had been so easily acquired. The truck exploded into flames and when the initial ball of fire and the smoke cloud had cleared he concluded that there couldn't have been any survivors.

He hurried across the pathway still smiling slightly with pride and met his unexpected comrades.   His smile vanished and he said, "Well, I guess we go it on foot now."   No one spoke and they picked up the gear that they thought they could carry and started walking.

Major Haffick rushed down the hallway spilling his coffee as he scurried along and almost running several people over pushed open the door to the surveillance room.   "What have you got!" he demanded as he entered the already crowded room.

"Sir, we're still analyzing the data but we found something interesting.   It's quite a ways south of where we have been looking and we really found it by mistake." said a young Airman while pointing to a large screen with a satellite image on it.

"What am I looking at?" asked the Major.

"This is a satellite photo taken at 18:23 this evening.   It shows what we think is an Iranian military truck on fire about seventy-five to a hundred meters from an American Red Cross van."

"I see, so what does this have to do with our missing plane?"

"We don't exactly know that it has anything to do with it.   You said to tell you about anything strange so......"

"Yes, yes, thank you, and dig a little deeper.   See what else you can find.   I'll re-brief the blackbird pilot in the morning and have him adjust his course to take a closer look in that area also."

"Yes sir." the Airman said as the Major walked out of the room.

As they walked Williams asked, "You said this trail leads to the mountains and that's as far as you know?"

"Yes, that's right."   Anna answered.

"Do you know how populated the area beyond the mountains is?"

"There are two main ranges.   There is a small village in the valley but the heavily populated areas are to the north of the village.   Then several miles south there are some scattered fishing towns.   Beyond the mountains it pretty much uninhabited until we get to another small range of mountains but even then it's just several small villages.   They should be easy enough to bypass."

"I don't exactly want to bypass them though.   That's where I'll need your help again.   And your clothes." he said looking at Mike.

"My clothes?" questioned Mike.

"Yes we'll trade for a while unless you want to go with her to get supplies?"

"That's ok.   You look about my size."   Mike said.

"You don't think we have enough supplies?" asked BB.

"Sure, for now but it's probably still a few days walk to the border. In this heat, we will definitely need more water."

"What heat?" asked Mike sarcastically.

Williams looked at his watch and said, "Mike, it's almost seven in the evening.   By lunch tomorrow........"

"Your right," Mike interrupted.   "I forgot it was that late."

"What was that?"   BB snapped looking behind them.

"I didn't........"   As Williams began to speak, he saw something move in the distance.   About fifty yards he guessed.   "Everybody get down."

He looked around for cover and found another large rock formation.   "Anna, you and Mike take Tami, and get behind that rock. I think we're being followed.   BB, will you help me check it out?"

"What do you need me to do?"

As Anna, Mike, and Tami made their way to cover, Williams said, "You go down and around to the left.   Try to stay low, quiet, and behind something if at all possible and please don't shoot me.   I'm going to the right.   The idea is to come back in from behind them, got it?"

"Got it."   BB said as he crept off to the left trying his best to be stealthy.

Williams worked his way back and circled wide to keep distance and moving quickly.   He suddenly saw one of the Iranians ducking behind a rock oblivious to the fact that he was being flanked.   The man was looking back towards BB's side but to far back to have spotted BB. Williams figured there must be at least two of them but where did they come from?   Surely they didn't survive the RPG.

He continued to move farther behind the Iranian trying to get a look at who he may have been communicating with when he first saw him.   He could still see the first man but couldn't see anything else.   His heart nearly jumped out of his chest when the shots rang out.   *BB*, he thought.   He looked up the one he could see didn't fire and was almost standing upright as if he was looking for someone.   BB stood and

Williams saw him at the same time the Iranian did.

"BB get down!" he yelled at the top of his lungs.   BB hit the dirt and the Iranian spun around.   Williams raised his rifle and fired.   The man hit the ground.   *Was he down?*   Williams staying low started to move toward the location of the man, looking for any movement.   The man stood up and fired.   Williams dove to the ground and heard a second rifle rattle off from BB's direction.

It was quiet, too quiet.

"Williams...........Williams.... You ok?"

It was BB thought Williams.   *He saved my life.*

"Yeah!   You?"   Williams replied.

"Yeah, I thought you were hit when you dropped like that."

"Do you think there was just the two of them?" asked Williams as they walked back up the hill.

"Yeah, if there was another one he would've shown up by now."

As they got back to the top of the hill Anna asked sarcastically, "Did you get the bad guys?"

Williams started, "Actually......."

"Yeah, they're gone.   It's safe to go on now."   BB interrupted as he started walking and slinging his rifle over his back.

As Williams stood there stunned, Anna grabbed her bag and she and Tami turned and followed BB.   Mike walked over and whispered to Williams, "BB took that one out didn't he?"

"Yeah, and blamed it on me, like she doesn't hate me enough already." Williams answered. "I guess there's no reason for her to hate him too though." he added as they caught up to the rest of the group.

When they caught up Williams stated, "It's getting dark and we're all tired so why don't we find a place to rest for the night and start over in the morning?"

"Do you think that's a good idea?" asked Mike.

Williams looked at Anna and asked, "What do you think?"

"If we get started early and as long as someone stays awake on watch we may be alright, and we are all tired." she said looking at Tami.

BB sat and began opening an MRE. Williams came and took a seat next to him and said, "You know, that was dirty a while ago."

BB chuckled a little and said, "Yeah but she didn't believe me she just thinks I was doin' what I had to, and she thinks you just do this all the time."

"That's just it. I've never killed anybody in my life until now."

"You could've fooled me." BB said quietly, looking up at Williams. "Maybe you just need to tell her that."

"Yeah, sure" Williams said smugly. As he found a good spot to throw his pack onto the ground he asked, "Hey, you want the first watch?"

"I got it. I'll wake you up in a few hours." offered BB with a slight smile.

He thanked him with a pat on the back and walked around to where Anna and the others were.   He sat down against a rock where he began to take his shirt off but the pain was too much.   Anna watched as Mike helped him get it off and she realized that his shoulder was hurt.

She couldn't stand it any longer and she asked, "Would you like me to take a look at that?"

Williams looked at her and gave a single, tired nod.   As she took the bandage off and noticed the bandage on his lower back she asked, "What about that one?"

"That one's ok.   It's from the crash.   Your Uncle stitched it up for me."   He flinched as she pulled the gauze off exposing the wound. "Sorry." she whispered almost not finishing the word.   The whole shoulder was bruised and was bluish grey.

Mike asked, "Is it infected?"

She answered, "It doesn't look like it.   It just looks like he needs to stop using it so much."

He gave her a look and said, "I didn't really have much......."

"I know." she said cutting him off.   "So, what makes you do what you do?"

"What do you mean, *what I do*?"   Williams asked.

"You know, like back at the camp." She said, as if he should've guessed.

156

"Oh, I get it.   You don't like me because you think I'm some sort of cold blooded killer or something.   Do you know what I do?   Do you know what my job is... in the Army?"

"What?" she asked, half afraid to know the answer.

"I'm a mechanic.   That's right.   I turn wrenches and change tires.   I don't get my kicks off of killing people but where we are, it's them, or us, you know?"

Suddenly, she felt terrible for how she'd been acting toward him and couldn't think of anything to say back.   They all sat there in silence and she finished rewrapping his shoulder.   She dug in her bag for a moment and handed him two small pills and said, "They won't make you drowsy but they may help lighten the pain."

"Thanks." he said and swallowed the pills down with the water he'd put in his cargo pocket for the hike from the van.   She walked away without saying a word.   He looked back at Mike who asked, "You're a mechanic?" in disbelief.

"Yeah Mike, I'm a mechanic."

Captain Ishbad was more than disturbed when he arrived at the Red Cross camp. He found that not only had his men at the Doctors' had been overtaken but it looked as if a full scale special operations team had paid a visit to his men there.

He called the General. "Sir, I think the American Lieutenant lied to us about there being only one left."

"Why do you think this?" asked the General.

"Sir, There's been...... Things didn't go as planned at the Red Cross camp. I'm going to need more men and I may need the chopper too."

"I'm beginning to worry that you are not the man for the job Captain. Is this true?" he asked with sarcastic concern in his voice.

"Sir, I will get the American if I have to go get him myself."

Not impressed with the captains optimism the general agrees to his request. "I'll have you three new teams at the Red Cross camp by in the morning and I'll have the chopper prepped and awaiting your order immediately. Captain, don't let me down again."

"No sir, I don't intend to sir."

"Good." the General said and hung up the phone.

CHAPTER 8

"THE HUNT"

B was finding it hard to keep his eyes open and decided it best that he wake Williams before he fell asleep on the job.   He stood and stretched his legs from where he'd been sitting on the big stony lookout.   He worked his way through the dark trying not to wake his sleeping comrades.   He found Williams and tapped his foot with the barrel of his AK.

"Wake up.   Hey man, wake up."

"Wh... what...what!   Is there some.........."

"Shhh, No Sarge.   It's your turn to stand watch and let me get some sleep."   BB whispered.

"Yeah, all right, just let me wake up a little.   I didn't realize I was that tired."   Williams groaned.

"It'll sneak up on you like that sometimes."   BB said, his white teeth standing out from the rest of his face as he grinned against the desert night.

"Ok, I'm awake so you go get some rest.   We're going to have an early morning."   Williams walked to where he could see if anyone was coming up the hill.   He thought of how hard it would be for someone to creep up on them with the moon as bright as it was.

"The sky is crystal clear with no clouds or bright city lights out here. Isn't it?"   Anna muddled as she sat down on the rock next to him.

"It's actually kind of nice, or it would be, if I wasn't stabbed in the back, shot in the arm and running for my life." He complained.

She stuck her bottom lip out a little and frowned.   Inside she really was feeling kind of sorry for him.   She looked at the moon or at least anything but him.   Then as always she looked at her hands and said, "I guess........I guess I owe you an apology."

Noticing the difficulty she was having admitting she was wrong about him he debated on letting her stumble around for a moment or letting her off easy.   He couldn't be angry with that face.   "I'll forgive you this time." he said with a half-smile.   "Just don't let it happen again, ok." and shook his finger at her.

She returned the smile tiredly, and in that instant he thought of his girls back home and tried not to notice how pretty she was.   For a moment it was quiet and she asked, "How's your shoulder?"

"It's been better." He said with a grimace.

She wrinkled her brow and tilted her head to the side a little. The moonlight bathed her face in silver and he was taken once again by her beauty.

"How's Tami holding up?" he asked in a feeble attempt to distract himself from the awkwardness of the moment.

"She's strong.   She'll be fine.   She has just had a lot happen in a very short amount of time."

"She and I both" He spouted.   "How about you?" he asked. "How are you holding up?"

"I wish was back at home watching re-runs of bad movies on the TV and eating burnt popcorn." She said with a sigh, and without taking her eyes off of the moon.

"Ugh.....why burnt popcorn?"

She gave a little giggle and explained, "Well I never could make microwave popcorn without burning it, so I just learned to like it burnt."

He chuckled and said, "Don't feel bad.   I can't cook either. Peanut butter and jelly is gourmet at my house."

She smiled this time with a tiny laugh and a squeak.   He couldn't help but laugh more at her mishap and they both tried not looking at each other to stop laughing.   Once they'd gained control he asked rhetorically, "So, you like children?"

She answered, "I love children, and I love working with children Anna has been one of my biggest encouragements.   When I was having a tough time at home I would just think of her and it would give me strength.   What do you think about children since you asked?"

"Well, I hope I like them.   You know, I don't just fix peanut butter and jelly for myself."

"You have kids?" she asked as if she was shocked.

He leaned back as if equally shocked and replied, "Yes, two girls. What, is it that hard to believe?"

"Well, I just didn't pin you as the daddy type." She whispered with a smile.

"What, Rambo can't have kids?"   He grinned again and she giggled.

Turning back toward the moon she said, "I guess you're right" and as she yawned said, "It's getting really late and I need to try and get some sleep."   She stood and as she walked away said, "Goodnight Rambo."

He smiled and returned, "Goodnight ".

Just before light the next morning Williams woke everyone.

"How long do you think it will take us to get to the mountains from here?"   Williams asked Anna.

"I think it's about ten or fifteen miles from here but I can't be sure." she answered.

"That's good enough.   We need to hurry though.   Those guys are going to be looking for their truck and I don't want to be this close when they find it."

"Hey Sergeant."   Anna said as she handed him his flashlight.   "I

162

think the batteries are getting low." she added with an apologetic expression.

"Where'd you........" he started.

"Tami found it...and... I think she used it last night."   Anna whispered.

"What if we need this light later and she's used up all the batteries?"   he asked angrily.

"Before you get mad....." she pleaded, and handed him a piece of paper, "I think she used it to do this."

The paper had a penciled drawing of Anna kneeling beside him the night before with her bag open working on his shoulder.   He noted that it was an exceptionally good drawing.   He looked at Anna who was half smiling and giving him puppy dog eyes.

"She asked me to give it to you."

"Me?" he muttered back.

"Yes you.   It is a picture of you."

"It's actually a picture of us." he noted egregiously.

"I think it's her way of saying thank you.

"Alright," he said folding the picture and putting it in his left side pocket. "I'll let it slide this time."

"We need to get going.   It's starting to get light." he said aloud without looking away from Anna.   She smiled and turned to go get Tami and her bag.   As she walked away she had the urge to look over her shoulder but she willed herself not to. Although, she still wondered if he was watching her.

As Williams walked away Anna and Tami hurried to catch up. As they walked, Anna looked at Williams who was looking straight ahead, deep in thought and she smiled. They walked past Mike and BB as they threw their bags over their shoulders and followed from a few steps back.

"What's up with those two?" asked Mike.

BB shrugged, "I dun no."

"I was afraid she might choke him in his sleep last night and now she's following him around like a little puppy." Mike continued.

"Guess they worked things out." BB said.

Mike stopped walking to adjust his pack and muttered, "It looks like they worked things out alright."

As BB walked, he noticed Tami holding Anna's hand and looking up at Williams as they walked. He shook his head slightly and smiled at the congenial trio.

The Captain paced back and forth as he waited impatiently for his requested reinforcements to arrive there at the bullet riddled clinic.

"Sir, the trucks are here." said the young Corporal.

"Get the rest of the men ready Corporal.   We must move quickly. They would've gone west toward the mountains."

"What about the camp Sir?   Who do I leave here to..." started the Corporal.

"Never mind the camp right now." Interrupted the Captain.   "I'll need everyman to get this guy before he makes it to the border."

"Yes Captain." the Corporal said as he rushed away to gather the rest of the men and get the trucks ready for the dessert pursuit.

The Captain knew he was in trouble.   The General was well beyond impatient and was beginning to get angry.   He had to find the American and fast.   He was running out of men and resources.   He knew that one of his best men was dead and due to the fact that the other had left the day prior and hadn't returned or checked in he assumed that he was dead too.

His last Lieutenant asked, "Why do you think he went west?"

"He will try and get to the border where he knows the American forces are." said Captain Ishbad.

"Sir, we are ready to move." shouted the Corporal from the passenger seat of the second truck.

The Captain turned to the Lieutenant and said, "Let's go.   We don't have much time."

As they approached the dirt trail that led to the mountains the Captain called over the radio, "Truck four, proceed north, to Arak. Check for any signs of them there.   Then make your way south back to the villages south of Khorramabad.   We'll meet you there."

"Copy that." crackled the response back from the rear truck and as the convoy turned off of the main road the last truck continued north to Arak.

Back in Balad, at the Airbase, Major Haffick splashed water on his face in the men's room and looked in the mirror.   "I have got to find a less stressful job." he said aloud.   He thought he was alone and was caught by surprise at the sound of a toilet flushing.   In the mirror he noticed his nightshift counterpart Captain Thompson stepping out of one of the stalls.

"Me too." he said.   "I'm only twenty-eight and I have more gray in my hair than I do anything else."

Major Haffick looked at the Captains hair and noticed that he was right.   He couldn't tell what the Captains original hair color had been because it was so heavily laced with gray.

The Captain looked at his watch.   "Why are you here so early

Sir?"

The Major answered while pulling a paper towel from the dispenser and speaking through it he mumbled, "I can go to sleep at ten and I wake up at three.   I can go to sleep at two, and I still wake up at three so I figure I might as well come on in and try and make use of my time."

"I see.   I don't quite have that problem but I work nightshift you know?   Besides, sleeping during the day wasn't hard to get used to since we're halfway around the world and if I were still at home I'd be on the same sleep schedule as I am here."

Major Haffick wadded up the towel and tossed it feebly into the waste basket on his way out the door.   The Captain followed him into the hallway and said, "I hope your day goes as smoothly as my night did."

"Thanks." he muttered over his shoulder as he dredged down the hall toward his office.   He unlocked the door and as he pushed the door open he heard someone calling.   He looked up to see the Airman from the surveillance room.   "Sir, you're not going to believe it. We found it."

"It took a moment to register and before he could respond the Airman added, "The plane Sir.   We found the plane."

Suddenly he came to life and said, "I'll be right there."   He ran into his office and realized there was nothing he needed in it.   He grabbed his coffee cup to justify going into it and returned to the surveillance room.   He handed the cup to an Airman as he entered and said, "Coffee, black".

"Sir, we found it about two hundred miles south of the Caspian Sea.   It's all broken up and I don't know about survivors but I know why we haven't found it until now."

"Why's that, Airman?" asked the Major.

"Well Sir, it's been buried."

"Buried?" he asked while wrinkling his forehead and raising an eyebrow.

"The only thing I can come up with is that the sand storm that passed through here the night of its departure followed it to its crash site and covered it with sand."

"How did you find it now?"

The Airman suddenly changed his tone as he answered, "We didn't.   They did." pointing at the screen.

Major Haffick squinted at the monitor, "That looks like......."

"Iranian military?" the Airman interrupted.

The other Airman had returned with his coffee and he took the cup without looking at the Airman and not taking his attention away from the Airman that was speaking.   He sat the cup on the edge of the counter as the Airman continued.

"That's because it is.   Judging by their progress we think they found it sometime late yesterday most likely.   That being said, we took a closer look at the area that we looked at yesterday, and look what we found."

Major Haffick stepped closer as the Airman pulled up a different image on the screen.   It was a satellite photo of a small camp that he guessed was the Red Cross camp noticing the red cross on the top of the truck parked there.   There were about half a dozen Iranian military trucks parked there also and it looked like there were about two dozen personnel standing around the trucks.

"What is this and when was this taken?" the Major asked.

"It was taken about an hour ago and........"

"Wouldn't it have been dark then?"

"Yes, but satellite imagery uses.....it can see in the dark."

"Ok, I see.   Go on."

"I don't know what it is Sir, but remember the burning truck and the Red Cross van we discovered yesterday?"

"Yes."

The Airman pulled up a third image.   "This is where all those trucks were about twenty minutes ago."

Major Haffick looked and recognized the van in the photo from the day before.   "Can you zoom out from there and make the image a CADRG (Compressed Arc Digitized Raster Graphic)?"   This would give him a better idea of where they were in conjunction to his location.

The Airman leaned over and typed on the keyboard.   The screen went blank and then came back, very much resembling a road map and this time zoomed out.   In the center, there was a small red square and the map showed all the country borders.

"Is that where we were just looking?" asked Major Haffick pointing to the red box.

"Yes Sir, and I zoomed out fifteen times from where it was."

He pointed to the red box and moved his finger west to the Iraqi border and asked, "About how far is that?"

"That's about three hundred miles Sir." the Airman replied.

"Thank you. Keep an eye on both locations.   I have to call the General and a few other people.   Keep me posted on anything dramatic."

"Yes Sir."

As he turned around everyone in the room started to stand but he motioned for them to stay seated and left the room.

As they hiked through the craggy foothills of the Zagros Mts. Anna asked, "So, what made you join the Army?"

Williams thought for a moment.   "I don't really know.   I guess I was always patriotic and when I graduated from high school I didn't know what to do with myself.   I probably joined just to keep from having to decide what to do with my life."

"I bet your sorry now huh." she said smugly.

"Not really.   I never thought I'd end up out here in the desert running for my life from some wacko General and his goons but...... That doesn't make me sorry that I joined the Army."

"I guess you think that's admirable don't you?"

He wasn't sure whether she was asking a serious question or taking a stab at him so he asked, "Do you?"

Surprised that he put her on the spot and suddenly lost for words she just looked at him for a second and said, "I guess."   As soon as she said it she thought, *did I just give him a compliment?*   She wrinkled her nose and brow at the thought and then tried to act indifferent.

Williams continued, "What made you want to be a doctor?"

With a sigh that turned into kind of a groan at the end she answered, "Both of my parents were doctors and because I wanted to work with children I decided on pediatrics."

Williams looked at her as if he didn't believe her answer.   Like there should have been a more interesting explanation than the one she had given.

Vexed by his reaction she barked out, "I don't know, I just did!"

"Ok, I was just asking." He said apologetically.

Realizing she'd over reacted she said, "I'm sorry I just......"

Williams interrupted, "You just had a really rough couple of days. I understand.   Even I get a little edgy when I've had bullets flying all around me."   Looking at his shoulder he added, "some of them getting pretty darn close."

She smiled briefly and quickly caught herself being charmed by his uncanny since of humor. She looked ahead and tried to fight the urge to look at him but she couldn't draw that image of his face in her mind.

She glanced at his face and he was looking right back at her. She snapped her head back forward and he chuckled at her shyness to his glance at her.

She couldn't help but find the whole situation amusing and trying to refrain from laughing she made it worse by letting out another squeak. They both burst into laughter at this point and after a moment they looked back at each other and there was a silent understanding between them that neither of them really understood but both accepted as they trekked on westward.

_____

CHAPTER 9

"DECISIONS"

A s Captain Ishbad and his men approached the smoldering truck he thought, *I'm going to need the chopper.* Looking around at the destruction he shouted, "One team move west on foot!"

"Sir it looks like they went this way." said one of the Captains Corporals pointing at the ground on the north side of the road.

"You take your team and track them. We will meet you at the base of the mountains." demanded the Captain.

The Corporal and three other men grabbed supplies and water from their truck and moved out. Captain Ishbad called the General and said, "Sir, it appears the American is using our own weapons against us. We found the truck that followed them from the camp and it looks like the American set an ambush for them with an RPG."

"Do you know where he is now?" asked the General.

"We tracked them headed west for the mountains. They are most likely heading for the Iraqi border."

"They?" asked the General.

"My Corporal at the Red Cross camp said he saw at least one other person with him, an American woman."

"Are you telling me that one American soldier and a woman completely incapacitated ten trained Iranian soldiers?"

"Well, Sir he may have special.........."

"I suggest, Captain that you do not allow them to get to the border." interrupted the General.

"They won't Sir."

As the Captain hung up his cell phone he considered calling for the chopper but decided to wait.   He knew they couldn't have made it to the mountains yet on foot and he would easily intercept them when they got there.

Mr. Patterson and another Pentagon Rep. were already in the conference room when the General and Major Haffick walked in.   Mr. Patterson and the Rep. had extended their stay at the base considerably longer than they had desired but were pleased with the fact that progress was finally being made.

As the General and Major took their seats the General asked, "You've found the plane?"

"Yes Sir.   It was located yesterday about two hundred miles south of the Caspian Sea.   It's right at the edge of the Dast-e Kavir (The Great Salt Desert) but that's not the interesting find."

He pulled a satellite photo out of a file folder on the table and slid it across to Mr. Patterson.

"What's this?" asked Patterson.

"This photo was taken yesterday of what we believe is an American Red Cross van and an Iranian military truck on fire."

"Do we know why the truck is on fire?" asked the General.

"Yes, and that's where things get really interesting."   He slid a second photo across the table.

"This is a shot of the same location just minutes earlier."

"Is that an RPG?" asked General Omar.

"We are working on clearing the image up to get a better look at the guy with the RPG and we hope to have a better picture by this afternoon."

"What about the Black Bird?"

"I changed his flightpath and sent him over both areas.   We should be receiving information from him within the next few hours."

"Where were these pictures taken in conjunction with the crash site?" asked Patterson.

"About two hundred miles southwest of the crash." The Major responded.

"And you think these photos have something to do with our plane two hundred miles away?"

Major Haffick pulled another photo from the folder and tossed it on the table.   It slid across the glossy finish and would have slid off the other side when Patterson stopped it.   The picture showed Iranian military trucks parked at the crash site.

"Mr. Patterson," Major Haffick said, "If the Iranian military is at the crash site and they haven't said a word to us about it we have to be suspicious of any Iranian military movements."

"Has anyone contacted the Red Cross camp?" asked the General.

"We have been in contact with the Association and they haven't been able to contact the camp, but they assure us that it is perfectly normal for them to be difficult to reach.   They also told us that there have been incidents where rebels would steal trucks or vandalize Red Cross camps but no one was ever injured."

"Do you think that is what we are looking at here?"

"I don't know.   I just don't see the Red Cross calling the Iranian Army for help with rebels."

Mr. Patterson cautiously sipped his coffee and wrinkled his nose at the discovery that it had gotten cold.   He put the Styrofoam cup down and asked, "Are you suggesting that we may have survivors that have somehow managed to hike two hundred plus, miles through a desert land and are fighting the Iranian military?   Do you realize how absurd that sounds Major?   First of all, the desert conditions alone would make it damn near impossible for anyone to walk the distance that you're suggesting.   Secondly, where in the hell would they have found an RPG?"

"Yes I know how it sounds but we still can't afford to take any chances." the Major argued.

Mr. Patterson stood and turned to the General, "Sir, I know we don't want to jump to conclusions here but if this is what we are seeing and Iran has committed an act of war, we will have no choice but to respond accordingly."

"We understand." answered General Omar.

Mr. Patterson turned toward Major Haffick, "Is that all Major?" he asked as he gathered up his notes.

"Yes, that's all we've got for now."

"Keep me posted, and all the same, I will be briefing the Secretary this afternoon."

They shook hands and once Mr. Patterson and the Rep. had gone General Omar turned to the Major and said, "I am going to put together a task force.   I'll have them posted at the border close to where those photos were taken just for good measure.   As crazy as it sounds, I would hate for you to be right and us be unprepared."

"Yes sir. Thank you sir."

"Are we there yet?" joked BB as they hiked through the craggy terrain.

Williams laughed, "Not yet BB and don't get too excited because once we do get to the border we are going to have to find the US forces before the insurgents find us."

"Well that's reassuring." raved Mike sardonically.

"Sorry. I was just being realistic."

The terrain was much different now and as far as concealment goes, it was working in their favor.   However, when it came to navigability it was proving to be less than agreeable.   Williams thought it looked like something out of a Clint Eastwood movie, only without the cacti.   He pondered for a second, the thought that he hadn't seen one cactus the entire time he had been there.

"How long do you think it will take to get to the border from here?" asked Mike.

"I don't really know.   That depends on how far we are and how difficult the mountains are to pass through."   He looked at Anna and asked, "Do you know how far it is from here?"

"I think it's about two hundred miles or so, but don't quote me on that."   She began to say something else when she stumbled and almost fell. Williams grabbed her.   "Careful.   You wouldn't want to sprain an ankle or something."

He finished climbing down the pebbly decline and offered his hand to her.   She considered insisting that she was perfectly capable of doing it herself but decided to accept his kindness.   He turned and offered his hand to Tami who looked at Anna for approval.   Anna smiled and said, "It's ok."   The loose rocks gave way under Tami's feet and she started to fall when Williams caught her and helped her back to her feet.

He looked at Tami who was wide-eyed and a little shaken from her near mishap and said, "It's ok, you're ok, I got you."   She clutched her drawing case close to her chest and avoided eye contact.   "Are you ok now?" he asked.   Tami nodded and walked to Anna who smiled and mouthed the word, *"Thanks."*

As he was attempting to traverse another unforgiving rock formation he looked up and noticed a cloud of dust rolling across the ground about a half mile south of them.   He could barely make out three trucks within the dusty mass and he recognized them as Iranian military trucks.

"Everybody freeze!" he shouted.

They all stopped moving and Anna asked, "What is it?"   Before she got the words out she noticed everyone looking at the horizon. "Do you think they saw us?" she asked.

Williams still afraid to take his eyes off the three truck convoy even though it was well out of their line of site answered, "No, if they had seen us they would have stopped."

"Where do you think they're going?" she asked.

"To get to where they are now they would have had to pass the van right?"

"Yes." she answered.

"If they know we are on foot but don't know how far we have gone since yesterday they are probably going to try and catch us at the base of the mountains.   That would give them the advantage of high ground."

"So what do we do?" asked BB.

"I think we are going to have to change our plan a little." suggested Williams.

"What do mean change our plan?" asked Mike.

"Well, if they are expecting us to go west I suggest we go south a few miles and then go west and just cross the mountains at a different place." Williams continued.

"That's a wonderful plan but it presents a different problem." argued Anna.

"Supplies right?" said Williams.

Anna continued, "The only village between here and the border is due west from here and if we bypass the soldiers, we will have to bypass the village also."

"What about the fishing towns?" Mike asked.

"It may be pretty risky to show our faces in some of those towns. They've been known for their violence towards American tourists in the past."

"We have enough food for at least two days right?"   Williams asked looking at BB and Mike.   They nodded.   "What about water?"

"We don't have enough water for the rest of today." Anna said sarcastically.

Williams thought for a minute and asked, "What about rivers? Are there any between here and the border?"

"Actually," Anna said, "To cross the river we would have to go south some but I don't know if we want to drink that water if that's what you're thinking."

"Well, it looks like the question is do we take our chances with the water and the fishing towns or do we attempt to go up against the Iranian Army?" Williams suggested.

Mike frowned and said, "If you put it like that the choice doesn't seem that hard to make."

"So, do we all agree on going south first?"   Williams asked.

Everyone looked at Anna and she said, "I guess we better save our water bottles then huh."

"Ok then south it is."   BB said as he carefully continued down the hill.   Anna continued down the next hill and Williams waited for BB to catch up to where he was standing.

"How are you hanging in there?" he asked.

"Up a hill, down a hill, up a hill, down a hill, I'm startin' to miss the damn sand." He paused for a second and said, "I'm tired but I think I'll make it."

"How about you Mike?"

Struggling to get his bag back on Mike said, "I would much rather be kicked back with a martini in Cancun, but considering the circumstances, I guess I'm ok."   Williams laughed.

He turned around and half jogged down the hill to catch up with Anna.   As he caught up with her he slowed to her pace this time next to her with Tami on her left side.   He looked at Anna and asked, "You ok?"

"Yeah, why?" she asked back.

"It's just, you haven't agreed with anything I've said thus far and I was wondering, why the change of heart."   He thought to himself, *is she actually warming up to me?*

Looking straight ahead she said, "I'm not stupid.   I know we have a better chance if we avoid the soldiers at all costs."

"I didn't say you were stupid." he protested.

She looked at him and did her little head tilt thing as she said, "I know." and smiled.

He smiled back and noticed Tami peeking around at him. "Well, hey there.   Are you better now?" he asked cheerfully even though he was far from feeling cheerful.   She snapped her head back forward and didn't say a word.

"She's a little shy."   Anna whispered and smiled at him again.

"I noticed." he whispered back.

CHAPTER 10

"THE DETOUR"

The current situation had made this particular Sunday more active than usual.   Even though the Airforce ran twenty four- seven operations Sundays tended to normally be less manic than other days. Many people took off for religious services.   Most staff and department commanders tried to give as many people time off if possible and Sunday was typically the day.

After the meeting with Patterson and the General, Major Haffick had gone straight to the surveillance room and that's where he'd been for the last two and a half hours.

"Sir we've gotten something back from the Black Bird." said an Airman.

Major Haffick shuffled to the screen to see.   "What have you got?"

"It looks like the Iranians are loading something into trucks at the crash site."

"Loading what?"

"We can't...really...tell." the Airman said, staring at the screen as if he were trying to make out the blurred image as he was speaking.   He gave up his effort and continued, "It looks like boxes or something."

Major Haffick looked around for a suitable gopher.   He picked an Airman that didn't look busy and said, "Go and get me a list of everything that was on that plane and bring it back in here.   I'm not planning on leaving this room until I find what I need."

The Airman pulled up another screen and said, "This is what we found as he flew over the Red Cross van.   It's actually about three miles west of the vans location but we thought it might interest you."

Major Haffick looked at the screen and could clearly see, two bodies lying side by side and four others standing near them.   He thought aloud, "It's amazing how much easier you can make people out on satellite imagery when they are lying down."

"It's still kind of hard to tell but if you have really good eyes you can make out that they are Iranian military and watch this."   The Airman punched a few keys on the computer and the screen changed.   It was showing the same picture but it was different.

"This is the same shot viewed with thermal infrared imagery. This shows us that our two Iranians aren't just taking a quick nap.   See how these are reddish orange and these two," he said pointing to the two lying down, "Are barely even noticeable?"   Major Haffick nodded.

185

"That's because dead bodies are cold and thermal infrared imagery sees heat."

"Have you been able to clear up that image of the guy with the RPG?" asked the Major.

"Not yet sir, but we are working on it and I think we are getting close."

"Just keep up the good work and keep an eye on these images. All of them."   He walked back to the screen that showed the photo of the RPG and stared at it.   *"If you are ours, how the hell did you get so far so fast and where did you get an RPG?"* he wondered.

The Corporal yelled to the other three, "Hey, come take a look at this."

The three came to investigate.

"It looks like three men and maybe two women.   One of the men is wearing tennis shoes so he must be civilian.   They turn south here though and the Captain is expecting them to go west."

"They must be on to us and are trying to lead us on a wild goose chase." said one of the men.

"I don't think so, and I also don't think they know that we are following because they have made no attempt to cover their tracks."

"So why do you think they changed direction?"

"Maybe they are trying to make it to the river.   They might not know where they are going themselves.   Either way the Captain needs to know."

The Corporal stood and pulled out his cell phone.   He dialed and waited for an answer.   After two rings the Captain picked up.

"What is it Corporal?" he asked.

"Sir, the American is traveling with at least two other adult men. One of which is a civilian.   And looks like two women or children.   They killed the Lieutenant and the Corporal.   It looks like they ambushed them with a flank.   They were shot from behind which leads me to believe that they are trained well and more than one of them knows what he is doing."

"Can you tell how far they are ahead of you?" asked the Captain.

"That's the next problem, sir.   I estimate they are a good ten kilometers ahead but they aren't going west."

The Captain gritted his teeth and asked, "Then where are they going?"

"They turned south, and like I said, judging by the tracks they are about ten kilometers ahead of us."

The Captain started motioning with his hand for a Corporal to round up his men and said into the phone, "Continue to track them and don't stop for sleep.   If they stop to rest and you don't, you should catch them by in the morning."

"Sir, yes sir." he replied and hung up the phone.

As Captain Ishbad closed his phone he turned to his men and said, "We're moving south.   We will have to cut them off at a different location."   He opened his phone back up and dialed it.   Like always, it was answered after the first ring and he said, "Ready the Hind for in the morning."   The answer came back, "Right away sir." and he hung up.

The Mi-24 Hind was a Soviet developed assault helicopter that the General had managed to slip past his government years earlier and had really not had a use for, but kept it just in case of a situation like the one they currently found themselves in.

The Hind was not simply a weapons platform, but could also carry a considerable troop load.   The General would send another full team with the Hind.   Due to its inadequate navigation and surveillance systems, the pilot and co-pilot would fly the aircraft but the additional troops would be utilized in the search for their targets.

As the Captain got back into his truck he said, "What is it the Americans say?   *They can run, but they can't hide.*   Well, let's see if they can hide from the Hind?"   He gave a crooked smirk and his driver smiled back as they drove away, followed by the other two trucks.

Mike gulped down the last of his water and said, "I'm out of water and I can't feel my feet.   How much farther is it until we get to the river?"

Williams stopped and checked his pack.   "I only have two more full bottles of water.   How are you two doing on water?" he asked looking at BB and Anna.

Anna checked her bag.   "I have three full bottles and a half."

BB said, "I drank the last of mine about an hour ago."

They were all out of breath and dehydration was peeking around the corner at them.   It was mid-day and the sun was straight above them.   Williams knew that they wouldn't make it the rest of the day if he didn't figure something out soon.

"Ok," he said, "We need to rest and wait until it cools off some before we try and go any farther.   Let's see if we can find some shade or something."

"Yeah," agreed Mike, "There was a cave right back there.   We could get out of the sun and heat for a while in there."

Williams walked over to Mike and said, "We're following you then Mike.   Where's this cave?"

Mike took them back about a hundred meters to where he'd seen the cave.   It was comfortably large and with a big opening allowed plenty of light and a dry breeze in.   The cave was unlike anything they'd ever seen before.   It was dry as opposed to what little knowledge Williams had of caves.

"I thought caves were made from water erosion?"   Williams asked looking at Anna who was the most logical reference of the current surroundings since she had been to Iran before and they hadn't.

"As best I can remember from what little history I know of Iran. This area was not always barren and this cave was probably formed years ago before it dried up and turned into a desert land."

Suddenly BB shouted, "Oh Shit," while stumbling and tripping over the bags in the middle of the cave.

"What the hell?" added Mike, standing in preparation for a hasty retreat.

"It's a snake over there!" exclaimed BB pointing at the back corner of the cave.   "And the damn thing tried to bite me."

"Stand back," Williams said while taking his flashlight from his side and handing it to Anna.   "Hold the light for me."

Anna twisted the flashlight on and pointed the weak beam into the corner.   She shook it and the light flickered brighter for a second. She thought to herself, *"Now he's really going to fuss about the batteries being dead."*

Williams remembered growing up in the country and catching snakes all the time and now he was going to have to catch one to save their lives.

BB grabbed his rifle, "I'll get that son-of-a...."

"No!" yelled Williams, holding his hand up. "That bullet won't stop until it finds something soft and this cave is solid stone all the way around."

BB lowered the rifle and Williams slowly positioned himself to the side of the hissing serpent.

"What you gonna do then?" BB asked as Williams carefully unslung his rifle. He held the rifle in his left hand and lightly dabbed at the snake. The snake lurched forward and as Williams was about to make his move the light flickered out momentarily and Anna shook it to make it work.

Williams quickly drew his hand back and gave Anna a look.

"Sorry, the light died." she said meekly.

"Are we ready now?" he asked. She nodded.

Williams probed the snake a second time and once again it struck at the intruding barrel when Williams swiftly grabbed the snake right behind the head. The snake twisted and thrust itself in an attempt to get free from his grip but Williams calmly took the snake outside where he walked to a safe distance, uncoiled it from his arm and tossed it away where it scurried into the rocks.

He returned to his amazed comrades and noticing there astonishment asked, "What? You've never seen someone catch a snake before?"

"Yeah, on the discovery channel, but he got paid for it at least." insisted Mike.

Williams took the flashlight and went back in the cave to make sure there were no more unwanted critters.   After he was sure it was safe he looked at the face of his flashlight which was sparsely glowing at this point and sighed.   "Well, it was nice while it lasted." he muttered as he made his way back outside.

"Ok, coast is clear." he announced as he exited.   BB and Mike cautiously made their way back inside.   Anna gave Williams a quiet grin as she walked past him and he felt a since of pride for a moment.   He turned and followed Anna and Tami into the cave.

Williams looked at the tired group of travelers and said, "You all need to take your boots off and your socks and let them dry out.   The last thing you want out here is to end up with bad blisters and not be able to walk."

Anna agreed, "He's right we have a long way to go still and while we rest we need to let our bodies recoup as well."   She walked to where Williams was sitting and loosening his boots.

As she started to speak BB interrupted, "Does someone need to be looking out?"

"Yeah, it probably wouldn't hurt.   I'll...."

"No you take a break I'll take first watch and you come get me in a little while."   BB insisted.

"Sure, if you feel up to it, go ahead."   Williams said.

"You were awake most of the night so it's only fair that you get the next break."   BB added as he walked out of the cave opening.

Williams pulled his boot off with a grunt and began loosening his other one.

"So, where did you learn the art of snake handling?"   Anna asked propping her feet up on her medical bag.

Williams noticed her toenails had been painted green but the polish was wearing off leaving the outer edges of the nails bare. "More like snake catching, not handling." he replied with a chuckle.   "I grew up out in the sticks and as a boy my summers consisted of running around in the woods and getting into as much trouble as I could."

"Where our house was, we were surrounded by water.   The lake was to the north.   The river was to the south, and creeks on either side. There was an overabundance of snakes where we lived and I was a boy that liked a challenge so I would catch snakes, turtles, lizards.   You know anything that would terrify my mother."

Anna laughed, "You weren't a military brat then?"

"No, my father was just an average, hardworking citizen raising a family and trying to provide as best he could for us. What about you? What were you like as a kid?"

Anna smiled, "I don't really remember being anywhere for too long.   My parents were always on the move."

"I guess that was tough for you as a kid, huh?"

"Quite the contrary actually.   I loved it.   Getting to see new things, new places, and people was great.   I had an amazing time traveling the world with my parents.   I wanted to be just like them."

"Well looks like you succeeded.   I mean being a doctor and all."

"Yeah, well following in mom and dad's footsteps didn't exactly include the tragic ending, at least not my version of the dream."

Williams remembered Anna's uncle telling them about her parent's death and suddenly he felt sorry for asking her about her childhood.   "I'm sorry I didn't mean......."

"It's okay." She said with a wave of her hand.   "I'm comfortable talking about my parents.   I find comfort in the thought that they died for a good cause, however small it may have been."

Williams reached over and placed his hand on Anna's knee and said, "I don't think helping people who are in need of help is a *small* deed. I think what your parents did was very noble and I think that your uncle was right.   I think they would have been very proud of you."   He looked at Tami then back at Anna and smiled.

Anna found herself trembling slightly, and holding back tears she whispered, "Thanks."

Williams decided to try and change the subject and said, "I've done quite a bit of traveling myself."

Anna sniffled and said, "Really?"

Williams continued, "Let's see, I've been to Italy, Germany, France, Spain......." he thought for a second and asked, "Oh, does Mexico count?"

Anna giggled, "Technically the grocery store counts as traveling."

Williams laughed back and said, "That is another reason I am glad I joined the Army. If I hadn't I wouldn't have gotten to visit many of the places that I have."

"What was your favorite of all the places you've been?" she asked.

"I would have to say Germany was my favorite. What about you?" he asked.

"I liked Italy but I will agree that it is a lot easier to get around Germany since they understand English a lot better there."

"So you don't speak three different languages?"

Anna smiled again and answered, "No, I speak five. I speak Spanish, French, Arabic, and a little Swahili."

Williams raised his eyebrows and said, "Impressive."

Tami walked over to Anna and Williams. She looked at Williams and said, "Did you like the picture I made you?"

They both looked back at her in astonishment and Williams said, "Yes, I thought it was a very good picture. I can't wait to put it on my refrigerator at home." he smiled at her and although she had no idea what a refrigerator was, she smiled back and said, "Thanks."

Tami walked around to the other side of Williams and sat down next to him.   He wondered if she was sitting there to be closer to him or if she just needed the light from the opening that was on his side as she pulled out another piece of paper and began to draw.

"She speaks very good English." he said looking back at Anna.

"Yes, she is a very good learner."   Anna said leaning around to see Tami who looked up at her and smiled.

"I guess the shyness is wearing off."   Williams whispered.

"I don't think she was shy at all.   I think she just wanted to be sure that you were trustworthy."   Anna answered.

"Well, I am sure glad she thinks I am."

"Children have a way of sensing these things in people."   Anna smiled at him.

Smiling back Williams asked, "What do you think?   Do you think I'm trustworthy?"

Anna knew she trusted him with her life especially after all he done for them so far but she wasn't sure if she was ready to give him that much yet.   She thought for a minute and said, "I'll let you know when we get to the border."

"I guess that's better than no huh?"   Williams joked as though he knew that she trusted him already.

Suddenly they were interrupted by BB storming into the cave

wide-eyed and gasping for air.   "There.... there.... there's someone.....coming!" he exclaimed.

Williams jumped into his boots and without tying them, ran to the cave opening with BB.   "Will they see us if we go outside?" he asked while trying to see outside.

"No, they are a good ways off but they're headed this way."   BB replied.

"How many are there?"   Williams asked as he walked outside.

"It looked like there were four of them." Huffed BB.

"Show me." he said chambering a round in his AK-47.

BB walked up the hill where he could show Williams their location.   As he got to the top he went to his hands and knees keeping low so not to be seen by the approaching enemy. "There." he said, pointing down at the four trackers who were pre-occupied with the tracks that they were following.

They are about two hundred meters out and we have the high ground advantage for another hundred and fifty maybe. Williams thought to himself.   He rolled over onto his back and said, "We have to take them out before they get to the cave BB."

"How we gonna do that Sarge?"   BB asked.

"We need to get to them without being seen and ambush them from the sides."

"I'm right behind you."   BB said gripping the hand grip on his rifle.

"Ok, stay low, and move quickly."

Williams slid back down the hill to the cave, stepped inside and said, "Everybody get your shoes on and stay here."   He handed Mike his 9mm and said, "If anyone tries to come in here don't miss and conserve your ammo.   There are only twenty rounds in each clip."   He threw the other clip to him as he headed back out.

Mike looked at Anna and asked, "Do you trust him yet?"

Anna didn't answer.   She took Tami's hand and moved to the back of the cave behind Mike who was trembling and trying to aim the pistol at the entrance of the cave without shaking.

Outside Williams and BB made their way through the maze of rocks back toward the direction they had come from.   Williams found a position that he was comfortable would work for an ambush and looked at BB.

Pointing at a large rock elevated above the small pass that they had come through earlier he said, "You get behind that rock and watch me."   He pointed at a similar position on the opposite side of the pass and continued, "I'll be up there.   When I nod at you start from the outside and work your way in.   The first two should be easy and the second two will be stunned and while they are still trying to figure out what happened we will take them out."

"Ok, I'm watching you."

"BB, If any of them get away we're screwed.   They will call their superior and they will be on us within hours or less."

"I gotcha.   Don't miss."

"That's right BB, don't miss."

BB climbed to his position and waited for Williams' signal. Williams watched the narrow flume where the four un-expecting trackers would be hiking through any second.   He could hear his heartbeat inside his head and thought about looking at BB but he was afraid he may think he was signaling the go ahead and decided to wait until the trackers were in position.

Just minutes later the soldiers showed just as planned but they were spread out more than he had hoped he waited for them all to get in the open and looked at BB.   BB nodded that he was ready and gripped his rifle tighter.

Williams looked again.   The first three bunched together to inspect the tracks the lead man had found. Williams decided they would not get a better chance.   He looked at BB and nodded.

Contemporaneously they leaned out unnoticed, took aim, and opened fire.   Williams fired first on the single soldier and once he'd fallen he noticed that BB had taken the other three by himself.   They both rolled back to the safety of their rocks and Williams quickly looked back to be sure they were all still down.

He looked at BB who was looking back and while pointing at him

Williams mouthed the words, "*You, cover, me.*" BB nodded.

Williams cautiously made his way down to the scene and checked that they were all dead.   He looked up at BB and motioned for him to come down.

"Get all the ammo that you can find and look."   He held up a bottle of water.

"They got water."   BB hooted.

"Yeah, BB, they had water; and now we have water."

They gathered up everything that they thought they could use and headed back toward the cave.

Meanwhile, back at the cave, after hearing the gunfire Mike, Anna, and Tami were petrified.   Mike was shaking and had given up on trying to stop it.   Anna heard footsteps and pushed Tami behind her while griping Mike's shirt.   "Someone's coming." she whispered.

"Just stay behind me."   Mike replied as he chanted, don't miss, don't miss, don't miss."

As Williams started to enter the cave he said, "Well, we have....." Mike opened fire three shots followed by one single shot and Mike yelling, "Ahhhhhh!"

"Damn it Mike, it's me Williams!" came Williams' voice from outside.   Anna sprang to her feet and ran outside to check on Williams.

"Are you ok?" she asked frantically.

"Yeah, I'm glad he can't shoot for sh......"   He stopped himself as

Tami walked out followed by Mike. Williams snatched the pistol out of his hand and trying to still be angry said, "I thought I said not to miss."

Anna couldn't help but let out a little laugh and said. "But we're all glad you did."

"Sorry." Mike said, not finding it funny at all.

"Don't worry about it. I'm ok. That's all that matters right?" he said, looking at Anna. She just smiled and started toward Tami.

Williams grinned and asked, "Were you worried about me?"

Anna knew she was terrified that he may have been hurt but she looked back and answered, "I'm a doctor I worry about everyone."

Williams frowned at her demeanor. BB interrupted saying, "Hey, we got water now."

"That's good." Anna said, still looking at Williams who was smiling again.

"Do you think there is any more of them following us?" asked Mike.

"I doubt it, but when they don't report in it will definitely raise suspicions with that Captain and this General Aveev."

"So what do we do?" Mike continued.

"There's not much we can do other than continue with our plan as we were." Williams suggested.

"So do we still stay here till it gets cooler?" asked BB.

"Yes, we still need to conserve our energy and water even though we have more of it now.   I'll take the watch this time and all of you need to try and get some rest."

They all went back into the cave and Williams climbed to the top of the ridge where BB had been earlier.   He turned around and began tying his boots when Anna came out of the cave and started up the hill. As he tucked his laces into the top of his boots she sat down next to him and asked, "Are you ok, really?"

"Yeah, I'm fine.   You were really worried about me a while ago weren't you?"

She laughed and said, "Don't flatter your-self too much now.   I guess you're not such a bad guy."

He smiled and whispered, "You're still avoiding the question."

"No I'm not."

"Yes you are."

"Ok, yes I was worried about you.   Are you happy now?"

He chuckled and sarcastically said, "What are you worried about me for?   I'm a big, bad, Army man, Rambo."

"Yeah right. More like a big, lucky, mechanic." she said back, and gave him an elbow.

"Oh, now I'm lucky huh?"

"We're still alive aren't we?" she said.

"And I guess that has nothing to do with my excellent tactical skills does it?"

"I thought you didn't want to be Rambo." she joked.

"Ok, that was cold.   Nah you're right, I'm just lucky but I'll take it any way I can get it."   He turned around where he could keep an eye on the direction they had come from and continued, "But I hope you know I plan on getting you and them safely across that border one way or the other."

Anna smiled and said, "I know.   Are you hungry?   I can bring you something if you want."

"No thanks.   Just get some rest.   I'll come get you all when we need to go."   He turned back around and scanned the horizon.   Anna reached out, rubbed his shoulder and said, "Ok,"

She returned to the cave where BB and Mike were crouched behind Tami at the only sliver of light in the cave.   They were watching her draw another picture, this one of the snake they'd seen earlier that day.

"She's good."   BB said.

"I know."   Anna replied.   "She will be a very talented artist when she grows up."   Tami looked up and smiled as Anna joined the audience.

CHAPTER 11

"THE JOURNEY CONTINUES"

"**S**ir, we haven't heard from the trackers in the last four hours." the Corporal said with urgency.   "What should we do?"

Captain Ishbad was growing impatient himself and knew that time was running out.   He must find the American by tomorrow or the General would most definitely be exposed.

As he finished his cigarette and thumped it away, he stood and shouted, "Start searching the nearby towns and villages.   Ask if anyone has seen any Americans or anything suspicious.   Don't mention anything about him being a soldier, just American.   Check with all the local police. If they went through any of these towns they may have contacted the authorities for assistance."

"If they are located sir?"

"Kill them.   Kill them all." the Captain growled.

"Sir if there is a child......."

Captain Ishbad looked at the young soldier and furiously yelled,

"Did you not understand my order?"

The Corporal stiffened. "Sir, yes sir."

"Get out of my sight now." he said as he turned to his other men. He threw his hat into the seat of his truck and with his nostrils flaring and his face reddening he yelled, "Find this American. I want him dead."

They all stood and tiredly began loading into their trucks to begin the search of the local areas. Unhappy with the speed of his men Captain Ishbad ordered, "Now!" his voice echoing in the nearby ranges to the west of their rally point.

The first town they came to was a small fishing town just northwest of Shahr-e Kard, the capital city of the local province. The Captain went to the chief of police in the small town and asked to talk in private. Inside the chiefs office he asked, "How can I be of assistance to you Captain?"

"Sir, we have reason to believe there is a dangerous group of people, Americans that have murdered several Iranian troops. My troops." he added for sympathy. "They are very dangerous."

The chief asked, "Do you wish me to help you in your search, Captain?"

"No. I only ask that if you see them, let them go and call me." He handed the chief a piece of paper with a number on it.

"We could detain them here for you sir."

"No", murmured the Captain with a frustrated stare. "It's too

205

dangerous to try and capture them here in your town.   We will arrest them once they have passed.   All you need to do is call me if you see anything understand?"

"I understand sir. I will have my men watching for them."

Captain Ishbad thanked him and took his men south to check the next town. The chief watched as the Captain and his trucks drove away into the distance.   He had a bad feeling.   Although he didn't particularly like Americans he was a fair man and believed everyone deserved a fair trial which was seldom done in Iran. Something was not right.   The Captain was not being completely honest with him and it was weighing on him as to what the Captain was hiding.

Williams had gotten the others up and they had been back on the move for about three hours.   It was getting dark and BB asked, "What's that light?"

"It's your imagination BB." grumbled Mike. "Congratulations you're the first one of us to see a mirage."

"No, I see it too." Williams said.   "It looks like lights of some kind. May be one of those fishing towns?"

"Have we really walked that far already?" Anna asked in disbelief.

Williams answered, "Yeah, we have been making good time."

"What do you want to do?" asked BB.

"What do you all think?" asked Williams over his shoulder.

"I say try and ask for supplies and safe passage." Anna said.

"We do have the girl.   Maybe they won't try anything if they see her with us." added Mike.

"Her name is Tami, and she's not just some kind of bargaining tool." Anna barked back.

"Ok, everybody calm down.   We all know that Tami is not a bargaining tool.   She may even be the most important person with us and it is important that we get her across the border safe and sound." Anna smiled at him.   "Mike does, however, have a good point.   With you knowing the language and her being native to this country we may not look as intimidating to them."

"So, we just walk right in there like we own the place or what?" asked Mike.

"I say we go in, if you will, *semi-tactfully*.   BB and I on the outside, Mike, you in the back, Anna in the front, and Tami in the center but where she can be seen."

"What if they think we are doing the opposite of protecting her?" Anna asked.

"We'll have to play it by ear and just see how it goes.   I don't have all the answers but I know we need water and we need to get to the other side of that town to get to where we are going."

Anna looked at him and then to Tami and said, "All for going in?"

Williams looked at BB and Mike.   They both nodded and Anna said, "Well, that was an easy enough decision to make."   Williams smiled at her again and started toward the dim lights of the little town.

The main path through the town was littered with rubbish. Everything was small and very close together.   To the right was what appeared to be the market and farther down was the police station which was clearly marked with Arabic and the English word, Police.

The street was deserted except for two figures one in the local attire consisting of a solid white robe and a red head cover. The other was in a blue uniform and Williams assumed he was a police officer.

"Salam." called the man in the robe.

"Anna replied with a smile, "Salam.   That means hello." she whispered.

"I know." answered Williams.

She wrinkled her brow at him and he said, "They taught us some of the basics but the only other thing I know is......."

"Awgaf te-ra ar-mee!" shouted the officer.

Mike ran into Williams when he stopped dead in his tracks.

"Yeah, that's the other one I remember." Williams said sardistically.

"What's it mean?" asked BB.

"That means stop or I'll shoot."

The men slowly approached them and Anna began to speak to them in Arabic. They exchanged a few words from a distance and then to Williams' surprise the officer lowered his weapon and smiled. "Ismee Jovar, huu-wa Oshamar."

Anna translated, "He said his name is Jovar and this...." she said pointing at the other man, "is Oshamar, the town Sheik."

Williams looked back at Mike and BB and said, "He's like the mayor."

They both nodded in understanding and Williams turned his attention back to the police chief.   Anna continued to speak with them and as she was speaking Tami tugged on Williams' sleeve.

He turned to face her and asked, "Yes?"

"They are going to help us." she said with a little smile.

Williams realized that she was as good a translator as Anna was and he said, "That's good. Thanks Tami."   He looked at Mike and BB who had heard and were smiling in relief.   Anna looked at Williams and said, "They had an Iranian Captain come here looking for us today and they say they think they want to kill us."

"We already know that he wants us dead." Mike said.

"I just hope you know what a risk these men are taking for us. They will be killed if they get caught." added Anna.

Williams glanced at the two men and said, "Then I suggest we get moving ASAP so that the Captain never knows we were here."

Anna asked the men something and they nodded as they spoke back to her.   The two Iranian men turned and walked toward the police station and Anna motioned for them to follow.

"Where are we going?" Williams asked.

"They are going to help us with supplies and they will help us to cross the river." Anna answered.

As they walked to the river Williams noticed that it was a very clear night.   "You don't get to see the stars like this at home." he said.

"It's because there is not as much moisture in the atmosphere and not so many big cities with bright lights to clutter the sky here.   It's actually quite beautiful here if the economy and the government wasn't so disorganized." Anna said quietly.

"I'll take the bright lights and moisture in exchange for not getting shot at every day." Mike stifled.

"You ain't been to Houston have you?" BB murmured.

Mike just looked at BB and kept walking.   When they reached the riverbank the older Iranian man said something to Anna and she nodded.   The man gestured for them to get into the small boat that was tied to a stake at the edge of the water.

"It's ok," Anna said stepping into the boat and offering her hand to Tami. "They are going to take us across and we will be on our way from there."

Williams leaned closer to Anna so not to be heard by the Iranians in case they really did speak English and whispered, "How do we know they don't just want to get us in the river to shoot us and dump our bodies?"

She whispered back, "You want me to trust you right?" He nodded and she finished, "Well this is where you have to trust me."

Williams looked back at the police chief and down at his rifle. It was loaded and the man hadn't taken his firing hand off of the grip since they'd met them. He looked back at Anna who held out her hand as to invite him to sit next to her.

He climbed into the little boat and the chief pushed the boat into the river and jumped in as it floated away from the shoreline. He started the tiny trolling motor and began steering the craft up stream. The opposite bank was steep and Williams figured they had to travel upstream to a more suitable place to unload.

The men spoke among themselves and Williams was getting more nervous with every word. He looked at Anna and she smiled at him. *"How can she be so calm with these guys?"* he thought to himself. He faked a smile back and peered toward the shore where the steep bank was diminishing and the edge of the river looked more suitable for the

LOST IN THE STORM

little boat to beach.

The chief guided the vessel to the edge where Williams jumped out and helped to drag the boat closer to dry ground. After they had unloaded and retained their gear the two men said, "maa el-sa-la-ma el-a-cuum."

Anna repeated it to them and said to the others, "They are saying, *goodbye, and peace be with you.*"

"We need to find a good place to camp for the night and preferably a good distance from this town." Williams said as he grabbed his bag.

"Yeah, if they came through here yesterday they may come back and just because they helped us, someone else could have seen us and we need to have some distance between us and them." Anna agreed.

_____

CHAPTER 12

"THE RESCUE"

The sound of the fighter jet duo screaming down the runway and up into the still dark, early morning sky woke the Major from what he called his habit nap because sleep for him never came in fully refreshing quantities.

As he forced his eyelids apart he could see the dim glow of his alarm clock across the tiny room as it clicked from 03:17 to 03:18. He thought to himself, *"What might today bring?"* as he twisted his feet to the floor. He attempted to crack his neck and stretched.

As he walked through the door the entire office seemed to already be alive and buzzing. As usual he went straight to the coffee pot and before he could even pour a cup he was interrupted by a young airman, "Sir, You're gonna want to see this."

Before either of them made it down the hall a scruffy faced Special Forces Soldier shouted from the other end of the hallway, "Is there a Major Haffick here?"

"That would be me." stated the Major as he motioned for the specialist to follow him. As they walked the specialist said, "You're

213

gonna wanna hear this." and he handed him a thumb drive.

As he pushed open the door to the busy surveillance room Major Haffick said "Next I presume someone will be telling me what the hell I'm gonna wanna say as well.

"Not exactly; However, the decisions made and the orders given in the next 12 to 24 hours may have more significance than any of us know."

Recognizing the voice the Major turned and replied, "General Omar. What brings you here so early this morning?"

"I received a message from the task force that some interesting information had been discovered about our……." He paused and with his fingers making imaginary quotation marks in the air he continued, "Situation."   The Special Forces guy spoke up and while pointing at the thumb drive said, "Pretty sure he means that Sir."

"Well, let's see it then." He said as he walked across the room to the screen.   As he plugged the drive into the computer the Airman began to explain. "Early this morning we picked up this footage." As he typed on the keyboard he continued, "Normally we wouldn't think much of it but given the past few days and what's been happening we thought it a bit strange."

"What am I seeing here?" asked the Major.

"It's a helicopter." started the Airman. "It's not what it is, as much as what type of helicopter it is, and it's location that is of interest to us though."

"Ok, so explain." demanded the Major.

"Well, Sir, This footage was taken just east of the last location that we tracked our guys."   The Airman paused for a moment and looked at the Army soldier as if to ask if it was ok to continue with him present. Major Haffick nodded and the Airman continued.   "This looks like a Russian Hind.   If that is the case it's very interesting because this model of the Hind has been retired and out of service for years." Suddenly the Army Specialist spoke out. "Hey!   Right there!   He spouted as he pointed at the map on the screen.   "Shahr-e Kard.   That's where this message came from that I brought you."

Major Haffick hurriedly sat at the computer he'd plugged the drive into and opened the browser to load the information from the drive.   He played the file and immediately realized that it was a poorly recorded telephone conversation in Arabic.   He motioned for his translator as he restarted the recording then paused it as they all crowded around the desk in suspense. The translator took his seat and began to translate.   "I am calling to report to you that today the Americans that you asked about today were here.   Oshamar gave them safe passage and took them across the river and into the valley west of the village.   They have……." The translator looked confused for a moment and then said, "He was interrupted.   It sounds like he was caught and had to hide the phone from someone."

After a moment they heard in a whisper on the other end of the line, "Salam, Salam, Jovar?" then a subtle click as the line was obviously disconnected.

As the Major stood to his feet, General Omar said, "I believe it's time for a meeting." He turned to the Army Specialist and added, "Get a message to your XO that his presence is requested….no….tell him that I am ordering him here ASAP."

The Specialist snapped to attention and said, "Yes sir!" gave a salute, and hurried out of the room and down the hall.

Within minutes the conference room was full and this time General Omar himself was taking the lead. "Ok everyone." He said as he closed the door and turned toward the rest of the room. "I will be frank with you all. The powers to be and the powers that be and those that are above me would likely assume that we just make this situation disappear. Furthermore, I am most assuredly acting on my own and without any input from Washington on this matter. What I know is that we have Americans and civilians in hostile territory and in danger as we speak. I intend to bring them home to safety. If anyone in this room has issue with that speak up now." After a short pause and the when General was convinced that there was no opposition he said, "Ok, first we need to pinpoint a good location for extraction. Major, that's your job. Get on it." The Major stood and scurried to the door. Just as he grabbed for the handle General Omar stopped him. "Major!" "Sir?" replied Major

Haffick. The General continued, "For lack of better terms, remember, this is a rogue mission. Any shit that this stirs up will most likely land on us and us alone." Major Haffick found himself thinking, this is the most alive he'd felt in months, maybe even years. Without hesitation he looked back at the General and replied, "Understood Sir. Perfectly" and proceeded to exit the room.

The General turned back to the rest of the room and scanned for the next piece of his plan.

Captain Logan London grew up just outside of Dry Creek Wyoming. Born a cattle rustler and raised a cowboy he was a true patriotic, badass, red blooded, American, Hero. He was decorated to the teeth and was known as the guy that gets it done when no one else can. His father had served under General Omar during the Generals early years as an officer and they'd become close friends. He had kept an eye on Logan for most of the Captains' career especially the past five years or so after the loss of his father to a brain aneurism due to a fall from a horse at his Ranch back home. The Captain and his team were also supposed to be wrapping up their deployment and headed home when General Omar came to him personally and asked if he would talk to his team and ask if they would be willing to take on an additional mission last minute. It was without hesitation that it was a unanimous yes and he was more than happy to take on any mission that might get him a meeting with "The Man" no matter what the circumstances were.

"Captain London." started General Omar.   "Yessir?" answered the Captain as he cleaned out from under his fingernails with his K-Bar Combat Issue Knife.   General Omar continued as he walked across the room toward the middle aged Captain, "I can give you three birds, one for transport, and two for support."

"Sir." said the Captain as he slid his knife back into the scabbard. "You get us transportation and we will get you the safe, successful extraction of...." He paused and leaned forward as he asked, "How many PACS?"

General Omar turned and looked toward the airman still sitting at the long conference table.   The airman realizing that was his que said, "As far as we can tell from satellite images over the past few days we believe there are five PACS."   The General turned back to the Captain who continued, "We'll bring em' home Sir."

General Omar turned to the rest of the room and said, "You heard me."

The remaining people in the room stood to their feet as he finished, "I want two gunships and one transport ready on the tarmac ASAP." Everyone gathered themselves and made their way to the exit of the room.

As the last remaining people trickled through the door and into the hallway General Omar turned back to Captain London.   "I wouldn't have asked but I needed someone I could trust."   Captain London held out his hand.   As the General grasped his hand he began to speak again.   The Captain interrupted, "Uncle Omar, Today we make my Daddy proud." He gave the Generals hand one firm shake and patted his shoulder as he walked past him to the door.

Williams shook his head in an attempt to stay awake and alert as he waited for the first slivers of sunlight to sneak through the clouds on the horizon.   As he picked up a small rock and tossed it toward a large boulder he heard the faint call from what he thought was a young child. He stood to his feet and readied his rifle.   Again and slightly louder this time, "Salam! Salam!" came the voice, this time waking B.B.

"Who is that?" asked B.B.

"I don't know," said Williams, "but I don't like it.   Go get Anna." He said without moving his glare from the direction of the mysterious voice in the dark.

As Anna approached the voice had become plainly clear.   It was a young local man; most likely from the village the night before.   As he approached he held his hands out as to show he meant no harm.   Anna assured them that he wasn't dangerous.   However, he did bring warning. After a short conversation with the man Anna explained that the Chief of Police had been caught by the Village Sheik soon after they had returned from the river giving up their location to someone on the phone.

"I knew it!" blurted Mike.   "We should go back and…….." "We should be grateful that they sent us warning." interrupted Williams.

"What now?" asked a worried B.B.

"I'd say we'd better get moving.   And he probably should take a different route home in case whoever it is after us meets him on his way back." Williams said nodding toward the helpful local man. "I'm quite sure that bringing us warning will not go over well with these guys."

Anna relayed the message and they all gathered their things together.

"Anna!" called Williams.

"Yea?" she replied as she struggled over a loose pile of rocks.

"How much farther would you estimate that we have to go to get to the border?"

"Hard to say but we should be able to make it in a days' time if we keep a good pace and we have plenty of water now." She said optimistically.

Williams looked back at the restless group of travelers.   He knew they were all exhausted but they had no choice but to push on.   As

Anna started out with Tami right there with her Williams waited on B.B. and Mike to catch up and said, "I'll take the back of the line today, Ya'll just look after those two." as he nodded toward Anna and Tami.

As they trekked forward through the craggy valley Williams contemplated what might happen if the terrain became too difficult for them to traverse.   He could tell that the valley walls seemed to be steepening and he wondered if he may have unintentionally marched his comrades' right into a self-imposed trap.   He tried to shake that thought from his mind and attempted to focus on watching behind them for anything that might look out of place.

As the sun filled the morning sky Captain Ishbads' men scurried about preparing for the days hunt.   The Captain stepped from his truck and approached a group of his soldiers.   As he reached their position they all snapped to attention as he began, "We will start at the river and work our way west through the valley.   Remember they are very good at staying out of sight so you will need to be very attentive.   At least two of them are believed to have military training so do not let your guard down. Remember, they cannot make it to the border.   The orders are as they have been.   No survivors."

As he turned to walk away his men dispersed to the helicopter and others to trucks. As the helicopters rotors began to slowly turn Captain Ishbad opened his phone and dialed it. "Sir," he began. "The Hind is lifting off now. I expect we will have the problem taken care of within the hour." The response was short and clear. "Do not fail." came the voice of the General his patience clearly depleted. As the Captain replied, "We won't" the sound of the opposite end of the line disconnecting was deafening.

Captain London thought how different the General looked in his combat uniform, rather than his dress uniform that they were all used to seeing him wear. As he approached the tarmac the Captain yelled over the whistle of the three massive helicopter engines as they finalized their pre-flight checks. "Are you riding along Sir?"

General Omar gave a half smile, "Not today Captain." He grabbed Captain London by the arm and added, "Watch your six kid. Remember you are essentially going into unauthorized territory on an unauthorized mission. If anything goes wrong it's all of our asses. We will be on a closed line of communication. You will refer to me as Papa Bear. The Apaches will be Alpha's-1 and 2 and the Blackhawk, Bravo-1. I will be the only lifeline you've got. Be safe, be smart, and I'll meet you right back here on your return."

Captain London smiled back. "Don't you worry Sir.   I've never failed a mission and I don't intend to start today, authorized or not."   He turned and climbed aboard the Blackhawk helicopter and placed the headset on his head.   He keyed his mic and began, "Ok boys unofficially, Operation Nickelback is a go!"   He reached over and gave the pilot a pat on the arm and with that they were off to the sky.

Unaware of the mayhem underway, the five desperate refugees of a situation that not even Hollywood could dream up fumbled their way through the rugged passageways on the Iranian desert borderlands. The sun had made its' full appearance by now and it was already unceasingly hot.   Mike was griping as usual about how awful it was and that they should've just stayed at the village and waited for rescue there.

"What about the Police Chief?" asked B.B. in an attempt to help Mike justify having not stayed at the village.

"We could've just taken him out." groaned Mike.

Anna chimed in and said, "By the time we would've known he was a threat it would've been too late."

Now, only miles from the border they had fought so diligently to reach, Williams hears the faint thump of helicopter blades cutting through the dry desert air.   As he pauses to be sure of what he heard he suddenly realizes that the sounds were coming from the direction they'd just come from.   As terror once again strikes at his very soul, B.B. asks, "Hey do ya'll hear that?"   Before Williams could thwart a panic Mike yells, "What the hell are we gonna do now?   We can out run a helicopter."

"Everyone stay calm.   We have to stay in the crevices and try and stay out of sight." said Williams as he gestured for them to get moving.

The three choppers blasted across the desert landscape flying low to keep under the radar.   As they roared into the valley churning up dust into swirling tunnels in their wake, General Omar squelches across the radio.   "Bravo-1, this is Papa Bear.   Radar shows you about seven minutes out looks like it's about to get hairy."

"Roger that Papa Bear.   We are good to go." responded the Captain.

Captain London keys his mic, "Listen up men.   Intel tells us that we may be heads up with a Russian Hind.   Remember she might be slow but don't underestimate her firepower.   ETA in five mikes.   Keep your heads on swivels boys.   I want Alfa-1 to take lead if and when you get eyes on, do not, I repeat do not engage.   I want you to draw their attention while Alfa-2 circles back on em'.   Once they realize they got a tail they will start evasive maneuvers.   Once they start evasive maneuvers Alfa-1 can return to Bravo-1 and provide cover for the LZ.   I want this to be an in and out boys, just another snatch and grab.   How copy over?"

Over the roar of the turbines comes back,

"Bravo-1 this is Alfa-1, good copy over."

Followed by "Bravo-1 this is Alfa-2, good copy over."

Once more Captain London keys his mic, "This is Bravo-1, Roger out."

As they cautiously scurried through the tight, crooked, passageways creeping ever so slowly toward their goal Anna with Tami in hand looks back to ensure the group is still intact.

"Hurry!" she exclaims as she almost tripped over a dried up dessert bush.

As Williams is about to respond, he notices the drop ahead and yells, "Wait!" as Anna, Tami, and Mike all three tumble down the steep embankment.   Instinctively B.B. and Williams both follow.   As they slide down this graveled ridge they tumble to a halt at the bottom of a deep valley.   As they survey their surroundings they quickly realize they are backed into a corner and suddenly Williams thinks back that this was exactly what he was afraid of.

"What now?" screamed Mike.

Anna grasping tightly to Tami looks up at Williams through tears and mouths the words, "What do we do?"

Suddenly the roar of the helicopter becomes louder and louder.   As they huddle together prepared to meet their certain end, the Massive Russian Hind emerges from above.   It begins to turn as the pilot spots the group conveniently deposited into a seemingly ready-made grave.   As the pilot readies his controls and starts to arm his weapons system they are surprised by the chatter of what sounded like an automatic machine gun of some sort.   Then, much to their astoundment an Apache comes roaring over their heads and turns south into the valley barely missing the behemoth aircraft hovering in their midst.   However, the Hind does not give chase.   Instead he steadied himself took aim and opened fire.

As the bullets begin raining down plinking and whizzing past the motley crew, Williams grabbed Anna, Mike, and Tami all in one swoop and took cover behind the largest rock he could find.   He turned to see B.B. taking cover as well.   As the chain gun rattled off hundreds of rounds per second throwing dust, sand, and chips of rock into the air Williams realizes he's got to do something.

"I've got to draw them away!" shouted Williams.   A terrified B.B. still ducking from the onslaught of gunfire yells back, "What do we do?" Williams repeats, "I've got to draw their fire away!   Stay here!" B.B. nods with a grimace.

Over the mic comes a disappointed, "They didn't take the bait Captain!"

"Damn it!" exclaimed Captain London.

"Alpha-2, what's your 20?"

"This is Alpha-2.   We are receiving light small arms fire.   We're comin round now.   I have visual on the Hind.   How copy?"

"Change of plan Alpha-2.   Fire when ready.   Alpha-1 circle back and give Bravo-1 over watch."

"Bravo-1 this is Alpha-2.   Just for clarification, that was a fire when ready right?"

"Alpha-2. Fire Damn it Fire!   Take that Sumbitch down!"

"Roger, Bravo-1 hellfire one, away."

Williams waited for a pause in the barrage of bullets, then, he made his move.   He stood to run and attempt to draw the Hinds fire when from the north side of the canyon, a missile came streaming through the air.   It splashed into an explosion of fire and concussion and the beastly, Russian war machine burst into flames and spiraled to the sand and stone below, eventually crumpling into a mangled heap of fire and steal.   As the burst of sound and shock from the explosion and crash subsided they begin to hear the subtle thump of the Blackhawk as it threaded its way down to the bottom of the sloped valley floor.

As the Army Medivac Blackhawk hovered there in front of them, from the dust appeared the figure of an American Soldier as Captain London shouted, "Are Ya'll gonna get in or stay here and wait on the rest of the party?"   As they made their way to the chopper Williams stopped and helped them all in.   As he climbed in and lay down on the floor he felt the lift of the powerful rotor as they took to the sky and back toward the safety of friendly forces.   As he fought to keep conscious he felt Anna take his hand.   Through sweat, smoke, and tears, and over the beating of the rotors he saw her smile and heard her say, "You did it Keith.   You kept your promise." Captain London leaned over and asked, "What outfit are you with Soldier?"   Williams just stared at the Captain who continued to guess.   "You with the 101st Infantry, the 3rd ID?" Williams just smiled and said, "275th Engineering Battalion."   The Captain gave him a strange look.   Williams continued, "I'm in a Maintenance line unit.   I'm a Mechanic."   He looked at Anna and smiled again.   She smiled back, looked at the Captain and said, "Not bad for a Mechanic huh?"   Captain London looked back at Williams and said not bad at all Soldier, not bad.

EPILOGUE

"Looks good on ya sarge." joked BB as Williams walked out of the examination room, referring to the sling draped across his shoulder. He was banged up and a little sore but the doctor had given him an otherwise clean bill of health. "Yeah now we match." added Mike, raising his arm just a bit, showing off his own sling.

"So, what are you going to do with yourselves?" Williams asked Mike and BB.

"I don't know." BB said. "I know I'm not going back to KBR. They can have that. I think I've had my fill of the desert."

"What about you, Mike?"

Mike was looking at his watch and was obviously distant. "What?" he asked.

"What are you going to do now?" Williams repeated.

"Oh, I'll probably go on vacation or something. Hit the beaches maybe a cruise." He thought for a second and said, "On second thought I might go on a ski trip."

"A ski trip?" asked BB with a puzzled expression.

"Or anyplace cold will do." he added with smile.

They all had a laugh together and then BB's face went serious.

"Well, I think it's time for us to go." he said looking over Williams' shoulder. "And you have business to get to." he nodded behind Williams.

Williams turned to see Anna standing across the hall alone. He turned back to the guys and said, "Yeah, I guess you're right. You fellows take care of yourselves ok." As they were walking away he added, "And keep in touch. I mean that." BB waved without looking and Mike made thrusting gestures with his hips while they started down the hallway. B.B. reached over and gave him a shove, almost knocking him down as they disappeared into the crowded hospital lobby.

He turned around and walked over to Anna.

"Looks like they fixed you up pretty good huh?" she said as she untwisted the strap on his sling.

"The doctor says I'll be as good as new in a few weeks."

"So, where will you go from here?" she asked looking down the hall and rocking on her heals.

"I'm not sure. I mean I know I'll go home to see my girls and all but....."

"But what?" she asked with half a smile.

"What are your plans?" he asked to change the subject.

"I have no idea. I already said goodbye to Tami and she is getting acquainted with her new foster family. I just feel lost now."

Williams smiled and said, "I have a suggestion."

"Smiling back she said, "Oh do you?"

"What do you think about... maybe... a movie or something?"

"Sounds nice." she said and stepped a little closer to him. "Are you asking me out Rambo?" she added in a whispered, sly voice.

He turned to walk and she walked with him. As they walked he slipped his good arm around her shoulder and said, "Yeah, I guess I am. I'll even make a special request for you at the theater."

"Oh yeah, and what would that be?" She asked.   She laid her head on his shoulder as they walked and he whispered, "Burnt popcorn."

LOST IN THE STORM

A special thanks to those who inspired, assisted, and supported me in the Writing of this Novel.

AshLeigh and Faye Willis

Mom and Dad (Wanda and Ray Willis)

Karen Willis

Kevin Minchew

Victoria Brown

Pam Tillman

Geoffrey Juday

Marcus Tubbs

KEVIN WILLIS

Donald Darwin

Walter Johnson

Amanda Williams

www.ingramcontent.com/pod-product-compliance
Lightning Source LLC
Chambersburg PA
CBHW072339030726
47501CB00016BA/1417